One Season

a novel

by

EJ Flynn

All characters appearing in this work are fictitious. Any resemblance to real persons, living or dead, is in tribute or purely coincidental.

For my Abigail.   I wanted to write a book I could share with you. Here it is. I love you so much. I love you the most. I love you forever.

Chapter One

I only read about a time when something called seasons existed. Winter, Spring, Summer, and Fall. That's what they called them. Now, it was always just Winter. It was always just cold. The type of cold that gets into your bones. This cold, we were used to. The ground always hard, and covered with snow. The sky, infinitely gray. Smoke from fires to keep warm filled our noses. Our bodies weighed down with layers and layers of cloth to protect us out in The Elements.

The chattering teeth, the uncontrollable shivers, it was how we knew we were alive. I couldn't remember being truly warm, but I know I must have been at some point. I knew the difference between what I felt now and what I once felt when my parents were alive. Maggie, my little sister, was lying next to me, curled up in a ball, clinging to her favorite teddy bear. She called it Louie. We had found it in a garbage can one day, when we were digging for dinner outside The Wilkes Estate.

I remembered that day well. It was an easy day. The Wilkes Estate was the largest in all four quadrants. They always had the largest amount of garbage. We did well there.

The Estates made up whole sections of land under large constructed, climate-controlled bubbles, keeping the occupants safe from The Elements we endured every day. Enormous, hulking, honeycomb structures sat like large bugs, guarding what we called home. A monorail system connected The Estates, creating a perimeter around us. There were smaller structures, built of the same material, used as utility buildings, the energy pods that powered the bubbles. People worked there. No one lived in them.

Those who were lucky enough to live inside, we called Staties. The rest of us, the unlucky ones living out in The Elements, we called ourselves The Community. I had never been in The Estates, never met anyone who lived in there either. We spent most of our lives hating them and their luxuries, while depending on their wastefulness to survive.

We were an overall peaceful society of people, living just to stay alive. There was some order established before I was born. People once took charge and tried to organize life out in The Elements, but it had since broken down to the simplest instinct of survival.

I looked around our campsite. The glow of our fire cast moving shadows on the concrete walls that surrounded us. I was able to take a couple of layers off, as long as I sat dangerously close to the fire. The heat warmed my cheeks. I could feel them flush.

Glancing from the orange flames, I looked at Maggie. She looked peaceful. Three heavy, tattered, wool blankets covering her. I didn't want to wake her, but I knew I would need to soon. It would be time to get dinner. I got up to stretch and get ready for my food run.

I peeked outside to see smoke from another campsite. Much to my disappointment, someone had moved in close by. I looked down in the other direction, only to see old broken down buildings and rubble, no signs of life.

It was hard to believe this was once a thriving metropolis. I knew only what I was told and the pictures I found from the past. History called it "the city that never sleeps". Now, it was basically dead.

"Annie? I'm hungry." Maggie looked up at me, rubbing the sleep out of her big brown eyes. She was ten years old. Our parents died when she was a baby, and I was only eight. I still remember the moment I was told. The oldest Pride member, I don't remember his name, we referred to him as one of The Elders. All the oldest Pride leaders were called that, out of respect, I guess. He brought me into his quarters. At the time, I couldn't imagine why. Then my whole life changed in four words, "Your parents are dead."

He said it without pause, without much feeling at all. Then escorted me back out to the main area where the rest of our Pride stared at me. Their eyes full of what I understood now was pity. They felt bad for us, a toddler and an eight-year-old, left without their parents. What would happen to us? I think my mind was too young to truly understand the horror of our situation, or to fully grasp what happened to them.

They had been shot by Statie Guards for trying to break into the Faulkner Estate, the only estate with a proper hospital, to get to a pharmacy. They needed medicine for Maggie. I remembered her being sick. I remembered how upset my parents were. But my memory of them faded every day. It was mostly just feelings now.

We never saw their bodies. Because we were so young, they were buried in secret by the other adult members of our Pride to protect us, or so we were told. Most people ran in packs made up of three or more families. We called them Prides. There were thirty or so Prides in The Community. After mom and dad died, we stayed with ours for a while, but with our parents gone, we were always an afterthought when it came to food or water, or a place to sleep.

There was a nice man there we called Uncle Joe. We weren't his family, but he treated us like we were. He was gigantic to me. Broad shoulders, deep-set almost black eyes, with a hint of sparkle when he smiled. He always wore the same heavy gray scarf. I asked him about it once, and he told me someone special had knitted it for him. I imagined his mother, or grandmother. His hands were rough, knuckles damaged and raw. He kept his hair short, but his beard long. His voice was deep and gravelly, and his laugh, the rare times we heard it, hearty and full.

We adored Uncle Joe. He taught me how to read, how to fight, how to scavenge for food. I spent hours learning from him, every moment I could. He took me exploring everyday. We walked miles through the ruins. Our favorite spot was The Great Library. He told me it was once called The New York Public Library. We dug through hundreds of piles of books. Dirt covered, tattered, torn, water damaged and crumbling. Still, we would spend days reading and learning. The other members of the Pride didn't like our relationship. Uncle Joe said they were jealous. We didn't care.

And then one day, he was gone.

I always wondered what happened to him. I had hoped to bump into him again someday, so he could see how Maggie and I grew up, how much we learned from him.

When Joe left the Pride, I didn't see a reason to stay anymore. I was thirteen. I took Maggie, who was only six, and we went off on our own. I'm pretty sure the rest of the Pride was relieved to not have us as a burden anymore, if they even noticed we were gone.

We did okay on our own. Better, even. I found abandoned buildings for shelter. I taught Maggie how to read, how to fight, and defend herself the way I learned from Joe.

I kept us on a very strict routine when it came to training and studying. We would spar against one another daily. Maggie was actually quite a good fighter, knocking me down more times than I would like to admit. I wanted to make sure she would be okay if anything ever happened to me. And it was nice to know someone had my back if I needed it. I showed her all the places I had been to with Uncle Joe. We didn't know any other way.   Just survival.

"Okay Mags, I'll go get something for us. Will you be okay here until I get back?"

She nodded, holding Louie. Pathetic little bear, missing an eye, visible threading where I had sewn him back together again. She was always fine with me leaving her. So brave and strong. I don't think I would have been at her age.

I got ready to make my way out of the abandoned building I had found for us to stay in. It was far away from The Estates and the rest of The Community. Most Prides tended to find shelter close to the bubbles, so they wouldn't have to travel far to get what they needed. I liked being further out, away from the crowds. People left us alone. Except, of course, our new neighbors. I scowled in their direction.

I set Maggie up with a couple of books to read, and threw a couple more logs on the fire for her. I knew she would pick her own books, and she certainly knew how to keep the fire going, I still felt the need to make sure.

"Be careful. I'll be back in about an hour. How long is that?"

"Sixty minutes, thirty-six hundred seconds and the time it takes for the big hand on the clock to go all the way around, if we had one this time." Maggie didn't bother hiding her boredom with my exit routine.

"Okay, make good choices!" I gave her a thumbs up, pulled my hood tight around my head, laced up my boots and ducked out into the cold. It was still light out. I had about an hour left before dark.

I passed a few campsites on my way. Most were empty; everyone was headed to The Estates for dinner. I had to think about what day it was, so I knew which one I could hit. Before I was born The Community had found a civilized way to take turns stealing from the Staties' trash, picking up their scraps and hoping every day they were extra wasteful.

It was the third Thursday of the month, which meant I was going to the Faulkner Estate. The site where my parents were killed. I had long gotten over the fear of going there, though it still haunted me at times.

This was the medical Estate. They were generally pretty stingy, and they served the blandest food, but that was fine for Maggie, who tended to react poorly to spicy food.

The Prides did a very good job sticking to the schedules. Most of the Prides got along, and interacted often. I didn't like to, and found it simpler to only worry about me and Maggie. I was better than most at surviving anyway. Other people hindered me. I was small, and it was easier for me to hide and escape. We had a few people try to get us to join their Prides, mostly because they could see how good we were at stuff. I gracefully declined. Maggie wasn't as quick to dismiss the idea. I reminded her there wasn't anything they could offer us we couldn't already get for ourselves.

There were thankfully only a few incidents where we needed to fight for our space, or our food. A teenaged boy tried to take Louie from Maggie once. Only once.

Watching my ten-year-old sister make a sixteen-year-old boy cry was priceless. We had established ourselves as not to be messed with, and people mostly left us alone. When our sites did get looted, which unfortunately did happen, we weren't there.

I made my way to the Faulkner Estate, the highest point in The Northwest Corridor. As I got closer, I could see the honeycomb structure break the horizon. They were like impressive beasts, lying in wait for their prey. Honeycomb, being the strongest construction, supported the acrylic enforced enclosure. The Community stopped trying to break in long ago..

My path to the Faulkner Estate passed old structures, pillaged for building materials. What were once tall buildings that scraped the skies were now piles of rubble. Everything went into the construction of The Estates. The pictures I found, the stories I read about the past, it was all impossible to imagine.

I found a place to sit and wait for darkness. I had my favorite places to perch, but liked to change it up from time to time. Today I stayed away from the other

Prides, hoping to jump ahead, get in and get out quickly. I pulled my hood and scarf tighter around me. The wind was picking up, and I knew it was going to be a cold one.

This life left a lot of time to think. When I wasn't reading or training with Maggie, I always found myself thinking. My mind would wander to a different life. Not the life of the Staties. I couldn't live like them. Even though they always knew they had a warm place to sleep and enough food to last them a lifetime, I never wanted to be them. I wanted to know what life was like before.

When I was growing up no one really talked about what had happened. Why those families lived in The Estates, and we struggled out in The Elements. I was eight when I found a pile of newspapers with Uncle Joe and caught up on what happened. I learned the tilt of the earth's axis started to change drastically about midway through the 21st century, and the seasons started to change. Climates all around the world shifted. Everything happened so rapidly. The world

15

was not prepared for it. Most of the earth quickly became completely uninhabitable, and it nearly wiped out the human race. The global event was called The Shift.

A

The majority of the people who survived were the super rich. They had the money to develop and build fully climate controlled dwellings before The Shift destroyed the earth. They started small, then continued to expand, taking over everything.

I was born after. My parents were still babies when it happened. They met years after The Shift, along with a lot of others. They lived among the survivors who weren't rich. They survived on the ruin that was left of the world. Why they ever wanted to bring children into the nightmare they lived in, I would never understand. And they didn't just make the decision once. They still had my sister, even though we struggled every day.

I didn't see a whole lot of hope around me and Maggie. We were simply surviving. Some tried to get work inside the estates, but the Staties were very picky about their help, and mostly employed their own kind. Generations of families grew up learning the trade and took over for the last generation's jobs.

So The Community stayed outside, and the Staties stayed inside.

Outside, suicides happened daily. Our kind was shot when caught, and there were no hospitals for us to go to. Some just simply went missing. Our numbers were dwindling fast. Every day we buried someone, sometimes two or even three in the same day. We were lucky to make it past thirty.

Once in a while, a Statie was banished from their Estate, for some reason or another, and forced to live out in The Elements among The Community. It didn't happen often, but when it did, they didn't survive very long. They either begged for forgiveness and were allowed to return to their Estate, or they died out in The Elements, lacking the skill or wherewithal to survive. The Community didn't have any sympathy for banished Staties. They were shunned from both worlds, and their stories never ended well. There was only one Statie who made it on the outside. Big John. I think the only reason he survived is because he went completely insane, and was reduced to his very basic survival instinct. I never actually saw him, but his story has been known in many forms by everyone in The Community.

While sitting in my usual spot, waiting for the darkness of night to make my approach, I heard footfalls approaching behind me. I sat motionless, hoping they would pass without stopping to say hello. I hated running into people. They would inevitably try to get me to join their Pride, or just chit chat, which was never welcome. The footsteps got closer and seemed to slow down.

"You're Anne, right?"

"Hi, who's asking?"

"It's Tanya. I'm part of the Amsterdam Pride."

I recognized her. She was older than me, but not by much. The Prides took their names from the street signs found in the ruins where they camped. Most of the time, if possible, that's where they stayed. Unlike Maggie and me; we moved often, growing out of our sites quickly.

I nodded at her.

"You don't have a Pride, right?"

"That's right."

"Why not?"

I rolled my eyes, I was so tired of explaining it to people who would never understand. She stared at me, anticipating an answer. I could only see her big blue eyes, and some curls peeking out from under the ear flaps of her hat. Her mouth, covered by a thick cloth, let out only a small amount of visible fog with each word she spoke.

"Look, I'm just waiting to get some food, and I really don't want to get spotted."

"Geez, I just wanted to know why, and I guess now I do. Jerk."

Her eyes squinted to slits, like an angry animal, and she stormed away from me, feet pounding loudly on the hard ground. I didn't care. I didn't care if people didn't like me or didn't want to be around me. I didn't like people. All I cared about was Maggie. We lived day by day, only needing each other. And that was fine with both of us. I *did* care about the abundance of noise she made stomping away from me.

I got up slightly, to see if I could spot where she'd gone. Seeing nothing and no one, I settled back in my perch to wait again.

Chapter Two

Darkness finally came, as my legs were beginning to cramp from my position. I stretched up, readying myself in time to watch a Pride jump ahead of me. It was Tanya's Pride. She must have actually been scouting when she engaged me, and told her Pride the best place to wait. I caught her looking back at me, as if to confirm my suspicions.

My face burned with anger. I could feel my eyes flare as I stared back at her. I knew I would miss my opportunity if I didn't make my move soon. I was about to jump up and attempt to salvage my approach, when I saw a flash of lights in the direction where they had gone.

Idiots, I thought to myself. This validated my reason for not being part of a Pride. The bigger the group, the easier to get spotted.

There were screams and voices. Clearly, they had been caught. I heard scuffling feet and crashes. Normally, some would get away, and I waited to see them come running back my way. I sat in the darkness waiting, listening for movement. None came.

I waited a while longer, then made my way to the familiar garbage site. The Dumps, as we called them, were made up of all the garbage from the Estate. Three gigantic chutes came from the bubble, each designated for a different type of refuse. One for paper, metal, and glass, one for food and one for textiles.

We were amazed and thankful daily with our finds. Staties disposed of perfectly good things. It smelled ripe. I pulled my scarf over my nose and started digging. I stuck to packaged foods. Things that were half eaten. It was amazing to me how much they wasted.

I grabbed a few containers without checking them. I would toss them if they were spoiled when I got back to Maggie. It was impossible to tell with the surrounding smells. I scored some half-eaten bags of crackers and chips, and a whole chicken I was shocked hadn't been picked up yet.

I loaded up my knapsack, closed it tight and slung it over my shoulder for the trip back.

It was unusually quiet. It was later than normal because I had to wait so long for the area to calm down. The other Prides were not out.

I climbed over rubble. There was very little left in the main arteries we used to get The Estates. The lack of people out was strange. I picked up my pace, suddenly worried about Maggie.

I found her just as I had left her.

"What took you so long?"

"Some girl distracted me while her Pride moved in on my entry point. Then they got caught, so I had to wait until it was clear."

"You weren't followed, were you?"

"Of course not, kid. You know I'm careful. Besides, no Statie is going to trek all the way out here." I winked at her, and she smiled. I loved that she still smiled. Looking around, you would think we would never smile. We found happiness in each other.

Somehow, in the darkness and hopelessness that was our world, we still found our way to smiles and laughter.

We opened the containers, and were able to salvage a few, and put the chicken over the fire to kill any bacteria it may have picked up. The good thing about The Elements was how everything stayed naturally refrigerated. It was nearly impossible for bacteria to grow, but we never knew how long stuff sat in the bubbles before being thrown out; it was better to be safe than sorry. Getting sick for us was not an option. There were no hospitals for people like us.

We set up our table, and ate in what I imagined was the way people once ate with their families before The Shift. We read about and saw pictures of life before. I always tried to give as much of that life as I possibly could to Maggie .

I set up our camp like a home. We had four walls and running water, and even a working bathroom this time. The space I chose was well intact. The street sign closest to us read G-a-n-s-e-v-o-o-r-t Street. I was happy to not have to name ourselves that. I wasn't even sure how to pronounce it.

Maggie was our decorator. She found tablecloths, and pictures, and old candlesticks, and made it even homier than I ever could have. I liked how comfortable she seemed here. I was pleased to have found a more permanent place for us. We had been there for six months, a record for us. Very little of what we had was ever permanent. Louie for Maggie, and a journal I found in the rubble one day when our parents died. It belonged to a girl much older than me when I found it. I read the words she wrote, and tried to understand them. She wrote about a boy she loved, who didn't love her back. She wrote about her friends, and clothes, and makeup, which I understood to be paint girls put on their faces to look prettier. She wrote about going out to dinner, and watching movies. Hanging out at something called a mall. All of it was so foreign to me. I kept her pages, and continued my own. I added more blank pages as I ran out. It was strange looking now. Tied together with remnants of leather I found years ago. Whenever I found blank or almost blank pieces of paper, I would add it. It was where I wrote all of my thoughts, ideas, and dreams. I would sometimes read back what I wrote, and laugh at how different my life was from the girl who started it. I would imagine what she looked like, and where she sat to write in it. On a big, fluffy, comfortable bed, in a warm bedroom with pink walls and a pink carpet. My version of life before The Shift had vibrant colors, and was always warm.

"Good pull today, Annie."

"Yeah, it was."

Maggie cleaned up our plates, and got rid of the little garbage that was left over. She came back and we played chess for a while, until it was time for sleep again. The chess set was made up of pieces I carved from stones. I was quite proud of it. Uncle Joe taught me how to play, and I taught Maggie.

I loved watching her get better at it. And the first time she beat me, she beamed with pride. After three very competitive long matches, I could see Maggie's eyes grow heavy. She left our table, and cuddled up on the bed she built from scraps we found around our site. I sat on an old stuffed chair we dragged from our old campsite. We surrounded ourselves with things we thought were special, or pretty. Pictures hung on our walls, some Maggie originals, and others we found exploring. I had started a collection of metal baseball bats,. if you could call five of something a collection. Uncle Joe gave me my first one. It was dented, the print on it long since faded. I knew next to nothing about the game it came from. Uncle Joe tried to explain it to me once, and we even attempted to play, which was difficult without an actual baseball. He signed his name on it, joking it would be worth something someday. It was definitely worth something to me now. The other bats had been left behind. This one I treasured, and I made sure it came with us wherever we went.

We would sleep in shifts. I knew it was probably not necessary, but with our new neighbors, it was better to be safe than looted.

I picked up my journal and wrote about what happened that day at the Faulkner Estate.

Hours passed before my eyes started to get heavy. I woke Maggie for Switch. Switch was what we called the time we took our turns sleeping and guarding our site. We traded out every 2 hours. Sometimes we would go longer if we felt okay. She was good. She never complained, and stood her post without falling asleep. We were well trained.

Settling under several heavy blankets in the bed I had built myself, I closed my eyes, thinking about the girl who distracted me. I already forgot her name. I wondered if she escaped, or was one of the ones who got caught. I hoped she was okay, despite everything.

Chapter Three

I woke to Maggie in my face. Her hand covered my mouth, holding one finger up to her own mouth with her free hand. I stiffened, and silently took her hand away. Her eyes looked to her right, signaling where she thought danger might be coming from.

I could hear people approaching. Maggie had doused our fire, and covered it to stifle the smoke. It was likely too late. If someone was coming, they were drawn to us by the fire.

"They're almost here," Maggie whispered.

"Get ready," I said, silently getting up.

We got in our practiced ready stance, back to back, our eyes in the direction of the approaching footfalls.

I tried to make out their size and number, based on the sound of boots crunching in the snow. I estimated at least three people. One had a slight drag to their walk, maybe a limp. One had a definite long stride, indicating height. As they got closer, it became clear there were three distinct gaits. Three against two.

Maggie and I tense, waiting for them to come around the corner into our site.

"They're right on top of us." Maggie's voice was barely audible.

I nodded. Our hands up, at the ready.

The crunching steps got louder, then quickly passed, fading away.

They walked right by. They didn't care about us. I breathed in, realizing I was holding my breath. I waited until I felt they were a safe distance away, then peeked around the corner to see them.

I was right. There were three of them, boys around my age. They were walking casually, without purpose. It was early morning, the sky a bright gray. I watched their forms grow smaller, until they disappeared behind the rubble.

My racing heart calmed. I returned to Maggie sitting on the bed where she had woken me..

"You okay?" I asked, sitting down next to her.

"Yeah, I'm fine. I really thought they were coming to loot us."

"Me too."

"I killed our fire."

"You did the right thing, Mags."

She looked at the ruined fire pit with remorse, kicking the charred, damp wood with the toe of one her boots.

"We have plenty of wood stashed, Maggie, I will build us a new fire." I put my arm around her, pulling her into a hug. I could feel her relax. She rested her head on my shoulder.

"Okay, let's get our day started."

We ventured out to see if we could scavenge for more materials. There had been murmurs of a coming storm. One greater than we'd yet experienced. We needed more things to burn, and if we could manage to find things to reinforce our walls, we would spend the rest of the day doing so. Our campsite was strong. It protected us from The Elements well. We had made it comfortably through some pretty severe storms. I never understood how The Elders knew a storm was coming. They were almost never wrong. They said they could feel it in their bones. Either way, the warning was always welcome.

"Annie?"

"Yes, Maggie?"

"I'm glad we have each other."

"Where's that coming from?"

"I don't know. I really don't know what I would do without you. Probably die."

"Mags, don't say that. You would be fine. You are smarter and tougher than anyone I know."

"You don't know anyone."

"Well, you know what I mean. C'mon, let's head back, we have a lot of work to do before the storm."

A typical day for us was filled with exploring, training and reading. I'm not really sure what others did to stay occupied. I didn't remember much of what the other members of our former Pride did. I only knew and cared about what we did. We had bright gray days, and dark gray days. The skies didn't give us anything else. Today was a brighter gray. We wandered as far as we could, timing everything to make it back before dark. I tried to gather enough food on my runs to last a few days. We were really good at stretching very little, so we wouldn't have to go every day. It was too time consuming and stressful. Despite Maggie insisting she could help, I felt it was too soon to take her, and her going alone was completely out of the question. I couldn't even imagine it.

Maggie had a unique way of looking at things. She was more in tune with our surroundings, much more sensitive than me. And she was very funny. I found her hysterical. She was very entertaining. Still full of hope and wonder. So very different from me.

We had about nine or ten hours of light per day. We spent daylight away from our site. Nights were spent finding ways to entertain ourselves. We sang songs we made up, and put on plays for ourselves. We wrote stories and drew pictures. It was a life. It was *our* life. Today, we stayed close to camp, so we could make it back in time to fortify our site for the storm. It wouldn't take as long, because we did a great job last time, and our site hadn't been looted since then.

Once we felt everything was secure, we sat for dinner

and Maggie went to sleep first. She had a rough day with everything that happened, so I let her go. Sitting close to the new (and vastly improved) fire pit I built, I wrote in my journal about the happenings of the morning. I would only admit in my journal how scared I was. Maggie didn't need to know. Soon, my eyes started to sting with fatigue.

* * * * *

I woke with a start. The wood snapped loudly, startling me, pulling me from a deep sleep. I was dreaming about a little girl. It wasn't Maggie. It was another little girl, from a time I didn't recognize. She had long blonde hair, pulled into ponytails high on each side of her head. She had a huge smile, and a gigantic rainbow-colored lollipop in her hand. I had seen one in a magazine we dug up with Uncle Joe. I was reaching out to her when the fire crackle woke me.

34

"What's wrong?" Maggie asked, looking at me with worry on her face.

"Nothing, I'm fine, the fire scared me. What time is it?"

It was still dark.

"It's early, you have an hour before Switch."

The wind was starting to pick up. The Elders had gotten it right again.

"Okay, well, I'm up, if you want to get some sleep."

Maggie looked tired, still shaken from the scare we had.

"Are you sure?"

"Yeah, baby girl, go ahead, get some sleep."

"What about the storm?"

"I think we have a while before it hits. I'll wake you if I need to."

"Okay. G'night, Annie."

"Goodnight, Mags."

Apparently, I had spoken too soon about the storm. It was right on top of us shortly after our unscheduled Switch.

Our fortified walls and windows were holding beautifully. Something large hit our southern facing wall. Maggie was quickly at my side. Our fire was strong. The reinforcements we made that day insulated our area really well, and it was actually warm.

The wind howled, and debris danced around outside. We couldn't see anything, which was preferable. Every so often, something would hit a wall, startling us. I continued to feed the fire. It wasn't close to going out, but somehow it made me feel better to tend to it. We would need it to last through the night, and maybe into the next, depending on how bad the storm was. If the snow was too high, we would stay in and need to keep the fire going. We had plenty to burn if we needed to; all the wood we gathered, amd pretty much anything we owned would burn to keep it going.

I peeked outside to see how much snow had fallen. It actually was not snowing, raining or hailing. It was just wind. I stepped out of our site, despite not being dressed appropriately for a storm. It was quiet. The wind had died down.

I heard a voice. It was a boy's voice, yelling for help. I assumed it was our new neighbors. I waited to see if his calls would be answered. I contemplated what I would do if they weren't. Would I leave Maggie and help him?

"Johnnie! Where are you?" I heard another voice answer him.

They shouted for a while, until they found each other, then it went quiet again. I was happy the decision was made for me.

"Annie? Are you okay?" Maggie called out to me.

"Yeah, I'm fine, kid. Coming back in now."

Chapter Four

It had been a couple of days since our scare from the three boys passing our camp, and the windstorm. We needed more supplies. We had used a lot preparing for the storm. I knew I would need to go on another run, so we didn't stray far from camp. It amazed me how there was always something for us to explore. Buildings and piles of rubble held treasure after treasure. Not only things we could collect, but so much to learn from. Books, magazines, newspapers, photos, paintings preserved by the cold waiting to be discovered. We uncovered a lot, Maggie and I. I always wondered why we were the only ones who cared to look. I guessed it was because we only had each other. The Prides had more people to fill their days, and entertain one another, and The Elders to teach them. Shortly after returning to camp, I got ready to leave again.

"Mags, I'm going to head out. Are you alright?"

"Yeah, I'm fine. Annie, I really wish you would let us

join another Pride. Then I wouldn't be left alone when you go on runs."

She was clearly still shaken from the encounter the other morning.

"Mags, we've talked about this."

"No, you talked."

"We're better on our own."

"I disagree."

"How do you know? You don't remember when we were part of a Pride."

"I remember Uncle Joe. He was great. And that little girl Cassie. She was my friend. We played, and had fun."

"We play, we have fun."

"It's not the same. She was my age."

"Mags, I need to go before dark."

"Hurry back this time."

"Okay, be back in an hour."

For the second time that week I prepped for a run. Sitting on our old tattered excuse for a couch. I tied my boots tight. The laces were starting to give. I would have to remember to mend them before they got too bad. I headed out, this time to the Taxter Estate; for some more food, and any supplies I could find. We were running low on most things.

I dragged the larger of my knapsacks, optimistic I would score a big pull. It was cumbersome, but could hold a lot.

The ground was harder today, with very little give, which made for a stealthier approach. I liked it much better that way.

Wind whipped around me. I lumbered along, weighed down by my layers, and my rucksack. Some of the camps had already started cooking their dinners. The scent of cooking garlic filled my nose. My stomach growled with hunger. Where did they find garlic? One thing I wished I had picked up from someone was how to really cook. We were fine with what we did, but sometimes my mouth would water from the delicious food smells around us. Despite living off of the scraps of others, their were people in The Community who knew how to make it taste good.

I dashed past a couple of the slow-moving Prides, shaking my head. Why did they feel the need to all go together? It made no sense to me. It simply slowed you down, and gave you more of a chance to get caught.

I spotted a group of teenaged boys ahead of me, looking for a scouting site. Among them were the three boys from the other morning. I glared at them, feeling my face flush with the memory. I recalled the boy in distress during the storm, assuming he was one of them as well.

Generally speaking, a good perch was high up, with a clear view of The Dumps. The boys were loud, and horsing around. They were undoubtedly going to draw attention to themselves. That was a sign for me to find a perch as far from them as possible.

I made my way to the opposite side of the The Dumps. The Taxter Estate seemed to produce the best textiles; clothes, shoes, cleaning supplies, blankets, towels, soaps, and detergents. Knowing we were short on supplies, I was glad it was Taxter's day.

Today, the site was guarded. It wasn't unusual. It WAS decidedly annoying. I had promised Maggie I would be quick, and this was going to set me back.

Darkness came, and I watched shadows move toward the site from all around me. I waited to see if anyone would get to the site without being seen. No one made a move. We all sat, waiting for the guards to go off shift. It felt like forever. Finally, the guards left their post, and the boys I saw earlier made their move. They scurried down the hill from their scouting site and disappeared from my view. There was a sudden flood of light. I squinted, shading my eyes, falling behind the post I stood at. I heard shouts, all male. Then the light went off, leaving the whole area black for a moment that hung there for what felt like forever. A single gunshot split through the darkness, followed by a pleading shout from one of the boys.

"No! Johnnie! You bastards!"

It fell dead silent. My mind went to Maggie. What would I do if that were her? The pain in that boy's voice sounded like what I would feel if I lost Maggie.

There was more commotion, and another gunshot. I imagined the boy who screamed, charging at the Statie who shot his fallen brother. I envisioned the rage that would make them attack, rather than flee.

Some more shouting, and then silence again other than the constant hum of The Estates,. and the whir of the monorail, which was all just white noise to us now. The guards were gone, likely having captured the other boys, and bringing them inside the Estate for some awful fate. I saw movement out of the corner of my eye, and knew my hesitation cost me my window.

I sat waiting for the rather large Pride to make its way down to the site, and slowly sift through for what they needed. I was so angry with myself.

I settled back into my perch to wait my turn. They were taking their time knowing the guards would be occupied with their captives. I would have been doing the same thing, if I hadn't missed my window. I was about to give up, and go home with nothing, when I felt a rope go around my neck. Before I could even react, a bag went over my head, and I felt someone tie my feet and hands. My mind raced. What could be happening? I heard voices as I squirmed and kicked. I could feel the bag draw deeper into my mouth, as I struggled to breathe.

"Get a hold of her, dammit!" I heard a male voice yell.

"She's moving too much, I can't grip her," came a second male voice.

This gave me hope. I kicked and wiggled more violently, and they dropped me. I felt a sharp pain on the side of my head, as it hit sharply against a rock or a brick. I felt the warmth of blood pool at the base of my neck. Suddenly tired, I desperately tried to keep my eyes open.

"Are you sure this is her?" I heard one of them ask.

"Yeah, it's her."

Then everything went black.

Chapter Five

I woke up to a bright penlight, shone in my eyes. First the left, then the right. I was afraid to show I was awake. I felt restraints around my wrists and ankles. I was on a bed, a real bed, and I felt something I hadn't felt my whole life. I was comfortable. I could feel a blanket over me. I didn't have piles of old ratty clothes weighing me down. It was warm.

"She's fine, a slight concussion, but she should wake up soon."

Good, they believed I was still asleep.

"Where did you find her?" It was another man's voice.

"Outside the Taxter Estate."

"And the sister?"

I tried to contain my worry. Maggie was all alone, and probably terrified, wondering where I was.

"She was way out in the barrens, the Meat Packing District."

My heart stopped. They had taken her, too.

"She left her there? Alone?"

"I have to say, they had quite a set up out there. They had basically a full library, a beautiful fire pit, a full set up of furniture and even working plumbing."

"Working plumbing?"

"Yeah, they found an abandoned brewery and somehow fixed the bathroom to work."

"Are you sure it was just them?"

"Yes. The sister actually put up a bigger fight. We weren't prepared for her to fight back. She kicked Sam and Jimmy's butt, until they told her they weren't there to hurt her, but to take her to her sister. She's very well spoken and well-read for a ten-year-old Common, and well, a damn good fighter."

"Really? That's extraordinary."

"Where is she now?"

"She's probably still eating."

"Has she been bathed?"

"Yes, I took care of that." A female voice joined in with the men.

"Dr. Kelly, good of you to join us."

"Thank you for asking me to head this project, Dr.

Sanford. I can take it from here."

Project? What was going on? I wanted to sit up, and protest, and demand to see Maggie, but I wasn't sure that would be a good idea. I stayed as still as I could, and tried to keep my breathing steady, despite the anxiety I was feeling.

"How are her vitals?"

"She's stable. Just the expected malnutrition, nothing that we can't get back on track quickly. Her IV will get her hydrated quickly, and then we can plump her up with a few good meals. She should be ready in a day or two."

"What about this one?"

"She's got a concussion and a nasty gash on the back of her head, because these idiots couldn't handle a girl."

"I would imagine she'd be a fighter. From what I've observed of her and her sister, they are definitely the strongest and smartest of their kind." It was the woman's voice again. Observing us?

The whirring machines that surrounded me seemed to

get louder, and I could feel a needle taped into my arm. The beeping got faster, and I realized it was mirroring my heartbeat.

"Is she dreaming?" one of the men asked.

"On the contrary," the woman answered, "I think she's wide awake."

I opened my eyes then. Four people stood around me; three men and a woman. Two of the men were young looking, wearing pants made from denim, and short sleeve shirts with collars. Their arms looked strong. It was rare to ever see a person's arms. We were always completely covered out in The Elements. The other man was older, and resembled the pictures I'd seen of doctors in a long white, thin coat. The woman also wore a white coat. Her brow was furrowed; I couldn't tell if she was concerned or angry.

"Do you know your name?"

I tried to speak, but my mouth felt dry. I managed to croak out my name, "Anne 24113."

"24113?" one of the young ones asked.

"Most of their kind don't know their last names, so

they were given numbers. Her sister is Margaret 24113."

"Where is Maggie?"

"She's in a room down the hall."

"Where are we?"

"You're in the Tyson Estate."

I knew the Tyson Estate; it would have been where I hit on Friday, if we needed more food. They were the second largest of The Estates. Calvin Tyson was the first developer of the climate controlled bubbles. He was an environmental scientist, incredibly intelligent. I had read all about him. People once thought his theory on the tilt of the earth's axis causing major climatic changes was absurd. The initial global warming theories of humans being responsible for the hole in the ozone layer was all people wanted to believe. When he introduced his theory, people thought he was trying to take the blame off humans and industry and development. But as time went on, his theory was proven, and finally, people started to listen to him. At that point, he had already begun construction on the first Estate. This Estate. Calvin Tyson the Fourth ran it now. After his first site was completed, he built the agriculture site over what was then called Central Park, preserving the lush earth in the middle of a concrete city. This was where the food for all The Estates was grown, farmed and harvested. It was massive, and the most heavily guarded of the bubbles. Slowly over the course of many years, the rest of The Estates were completed.

"Why am I here?"

"Anne, you have to rest. I promise everything will be explained to you."

I looked up at her. She was pretty, younger than I imagined a doctor to be. Red hair and green eyes. The pale skin of her long neck almost glowed in the bright artificial light. I saw her pull something out of her pocket, a long needle. I prepared for pain to follow, but she injected it into the needle in my arm they kept calling an IV instead. I had so many questions I wanted to ask, but I suddenly felt extremely sleepy. My vision sloshed about like water in a glass. I couldn't keep my eyes open or form words.

Chapter Six

When I woke up again, I was alone in the room. I felt much better. My wrists and ankles were no longer chained to the bed. The IV was still attached to my arm, and the machines were still beeping and whirring around me.

I sat up expecting to feel dizzy, but I didn't. I actually felt better than I ever had before. I looked around the room. It was stark white. No windows, only a single door, with no doorknob. I was dressed in a white shirt and pants. I felt truly clean for the first time. I looked down at my hands. They looked strange to me. I could see a distorted reflection of myself in one of the machines. The person looking back at me was a stranger. I touched my face, then my hair. It was brown, long and tangle free. I could see my face. It didn't look as pale as it normally did. My eyes looked huge, and bright blue. I had no memory of ever seeing myself that way.

`Looking around again, I saw what looked like a small

camera mounted in the far corner of the room pointing right at me. They were watching me.

"Anne, are you alright?"

A female voice came from above. It sounded tinny. I looked up to see a white disc with perfectly even-sized holes cut out of it, flush in the ceiling above me.

"I want to see my sister." I found my voice again.

"You will."

"Now! What are we doing here? What do you want from us?"

I jumped off the bed, and pulled the IV from my arm. Ignoring the pain, I pulled off the rest of the wires attached to me, and the machines started to beep erratically. One went to a long steady tone. I ran to the door, trying to figure out how to open it. There was nothing. No button, handle, nothing.

"Let me out of here!" I started screaming and banging on the door. I grabbed the pole my IV was attached to and trashed the camera.

"Anne, calm down."

"Screw you! Let me out of here! I want my sister!"

"Anne, please calm down."

I started knocking over machines, and throwing anything I could find at the door.

Finally, the door opened and a man dressed all in white, armed with another large needle, walked in. His hair was short, he had a beard and mustache. He looked like a bull. I threw a glass bottle with little white gauzy pieces of cloth in it. It caught him square on the forehead. The glass shattered, and he stumbled backward. He wiped the blood from his head, but kept coming toward me, looking much angrier.

I grabbed a bigger glass jar. with long cotton swabs in it, and hurled it at him. Again, I caught him in the head, this time the glass not breaking until it hit the ground. He went down with a grunt. He dropped the needle and it shattered into a bunch of tiny pieces, its liquid contents pooling in a puddle next to him.

The door was still open. I ran passed him, carefully avoiding the broken glass with my bare feet, and out the door. It led to a long hallway, with doors on either side. Each marked with a name. George 12118, Mary

11177, Margaret 24113. I stopped and tried to figure out how to open Maggie's door. An alarm sounded, and bright lights flashed above me. I ran back to the room, where the damaged man lay on the floor. He started to wake up, pushing himself up onto all fours. I pushed one of the larger machines over onto his head. He fell back flat, face down on the floor, limp. Searching him, I found what looked like a fat key in his pocket. I grabbed it, and ran back to Maggie's room. I waved the strange key around, until the door slid open. Maggie was sitting on a bed, dressed identically to me. She looked to be drawing or coloring. She appeared surprisingly happy.

"Annie! Hi!" She looked up and smiled at me.

"Come on, baby, we have to get out of here."

"What? Why?"

"We're not supposed to be here. You hear those alarms? They're coming for us; we have to go."

"Anne, please stop. You're not going anywhere." The same voice came from above.

I picked up Maggie's IV pole and trashed the camera

in her room. I grabbed her hand and pulled her off her bed and out the door.

"Annie stop! I don't want to leave here!"

Maggie was pulling me back.

"Mags, these are not good people. They want to hurt us."

"What are you talking about? They've given me food, so much food, and these clothes and a bed to sleep in."

"Why would they do that Mags?"

She shrugged. I picked her up, not wanting to argue anymore. I felt stronger than I had ever felt before. Stronger and faster. I ran down the hall with her in my arms. She protested the entire time. All I could think about was getting out.

Two more men appeared at the end of the hallway. I turned right, and ran down another hallway. There was a door marked "Emergency Exit" at the end of this one. Maggie felt light as a feather in my arms. I was at the door much faster than I expected. I waved the strange key around, and the door slid open. Outside wasn't the outside I was expecting. I braced myself, expecting to be met with the whipping wind and cold we were used to. Instead, we stepped out into nothing I had ever experienced before.

It was nighttime. I could see stars above us. We were in a street. An immaculately clean, smooth-surfaced street. I put Maggie down, and grabbed her hand. We ran down the deserted street. I felt like we were glowing in our white clothes. I looked behind us, and it was as if the building we just came from had disappeared. On either side of the street were darkened windows with beautiful clothes and shiny items. I had heard about what the inside of these bubbles looked like, but could never really comprehend it. The buildings were short, no higher than three stories. Most windows were dark, only a speckled few lit ones lined the streets.

"Annie, where are we going? Why did you take me out here?"

I knelt down in front of her, holding her hands, "Mags, these people have kidnapped us. When they took me they tied me up and put a bag over my head. How did they get you?"

"They told me you were hurt, and said they would bring me to you. You were gone so long, I was worried and scared."

"How long was I gone before they came for you?"

"I don't know. You said you were going for an hour, and it was much longer than that."

"Maggie, listen to me. These people are dangerous. I don't know what they want from us, but anybody that needs to tie me up doesn't want to help us. Do you understand?"

"But they didn't hurt me. They bathed me, fed me and gave me clothes. I feel so good. It's a hospital, they're healing us."

"Do you trust me, Mags?"

"Of course."

"Then you have to listen to me."

I knew she wasn't convinced; she wanted to get back to her coloring, but she followed me anyway.

We crept down the street, trying to keep to the shadows. Miraculously, we didn't seem to be followed. I needed to get us some shoes, and other clothes, for when we made it out of the bubble. Everything was so clean. There was no garbage to rummage through.

"Annie, are you bringing us back out there?"

"Mags, we have to get out of here. This is the Tyson Estate. That was not a hospital we were in. The Faulkner Estate is the only one with a hospital, remember? We need to get as far away from here as we can."

We saw a light coming towards us from down the street, where we had just run from. I grabbed Maggie's hand, and we ran down an alley between two buildings. It was so strange to not feel dirt or snow under my feet. It was then I realized we had been running for a while, yet neither of us were winded. I didn't even feel like my heart was beating fast. Maggie was right. I felt really good too. What had they done to us in there?

The light passed, and we crept back out to the main road.

"Annie, look out!"

Somebody tried to grab me from behind. I ducked, and they rolled over me. Maggie gave him a swift kick in the head with the heel of her foot. I leapt on top of him, quickly searching him for a weapon. Maggie had moved into defense position, covering my back. I wrapped my arm around his neck, applying enough pressure to keep him down. My knee was jammed into the middle of his back.

"Are you alone?"

I loosened my grip enough to allow him to nod.

"What do you want from us?"

"Everything."

"What?"

"We need you to come back to The Combine."

"Why?"

"Annie, somebody's coming," Maggie said still in defense position.

"You said you were alone."

We were suddenly surrounded. We fought ferociously, until they overpowered us in number.

We were both flanked by men dressed in black, both of us bloodied from the fight. A vehicle pulled up, and Dr. Kelly got out.

"Anne, it's very important for you to come back to The Combine. It's not safe for you out here."

"I don't think it will be safe to come with you."

I looked at Maggie. She didn't look scared. She looked relieved. She wanted to go back. She liked the warmth, and the endless amounts of food. I couldn't really blame her. But I also knew that there was nothing right about what was happening to us. At the same time, there was no way we were going to escape. There were too many of them.

"Anne, we need to get you back to the lab. I will explain everything to you when we get there, I promise."

We had no choice. This battle was lost. I would have to find another opportunity. We conceded, and went back with them.

Chapter Seven

They didn't restrain us, but they took us back in separate cars, despite our protests. The seats were made of leather, immaculately clean. Running my hand over the soft leather seat, I breathed in unfamiliar smells. I refused to speak the entire ride back, and hoped Maggie would do the same. I stared out the window, surprised at how much ground Maggie and I had covered so quickly. We passed the short buildings and immaculate streets. Not a soul was out. My inner clock told me it was somewhere around 10:00 PM, a bit early for everyone to be home in bed. I had so many questions, but I didn't want to give them the satisfaction of conversation.

I looked down at my hands. I could swear I had cut one of them on the face of one the guys who jumped us. There was no wound. I felt my lip, where a solid punch or elbow had landed. Dried blood, no cut. My mind was racing with questions. What were they doing to us in that lab?

We finally arrived, and were escorted to a different room. A large room, made up to look like a real home.

"What's this?" Maggie asked, wide-eyed.

"This is where you and Anne will be staying."

Still, I said nothing. Maggie bounced in, and started touching and playing with everything and anything she could get her hands on. She ran into one of the bedrooms.

"I pick this one, Annie!"

I smiled at her, then scowled at Dr. Kelly, who was still standing in the doorway, looking too pleased in my opinion.

"Anne, I promise you will be happy here, and everything will be explained in due time."

"Whatever."

She closed the door, and I looked around for the cameras I knew were hidden throughout our fake, new home.

"Annie, I want Louie."

I hadn't even thought about all the supplies and things

we left behind. My books, and journals, and pictures that Maggie drew for me, the life we'd collected and made for ourselves over the past eight years since we'd been on our own. Just as I was about to try to figure out how to call for someone, the door opened and a disinterested young man came in, pushing a cart full of the contents of our makeshift home out in The Elements. Everything was there, including my signed baseball bat from Uncle Joe. Louie sat atop it all. Maggie squealed with delight, seeing her favorite bear.

I looked around again, searching for the cameras and microphones. Refusing to believe it was simply a coincidence, it unsettled me that they knew what Maggie said, and were on the ready to bring it in to us. I waited for the delivery boy to leave, and dove into the pile. Everything that mattered was there. I picked up my tattered journal. It was banded closed, but looked to have been recently opened. Somebody had read it. I wasn't surprised. Why wouldn't they violate every aspect of our lives? I scanned the rest, and picked out what I wanted to keep, leaning Uncle Joe's bat in the corner, as I walked into the room that Maggie hadn't picked. It was stocked with everything I could possibly need, and then some. There were clothes hanging in the closet that I assumed would fit me perfectly, a row of shoes in every style. If I were anyone else from The Community, I would be thrilled to find a closet like it. I was not thrilled, or impressed. I was suspicious of everything, and I wanted to know why we were there. It was clearly not out of the kindness of their hearts to take us in out of The Elements. They had plans for us, and I knew it wasn't good.

A voice from above told us we should try to get some sleep. Maggie was already asleep, smiling and hugging Louie. I settled into my bed. I had to admit, it was comfortable. Everything smelled clean, and looked deliberately normal, at least *someone's* normal. I was suddenly exhausted. Closing my eyes, I fell asleep a lot faster than I thought I would.

Chapter Eight

The next morning, we found out what our routine would be. A persistent ringing sound came from above, waking us up at precisely 7:00 AM. Maggie was quickly in my room following it. A knock at the door was next. We didn't open it. A man's voice, muffled but audible said, "You need to begin your day. Please dress in the white clothes in the top drawers of your respective bedroom dressers. I will wait for you out here, to escort you to your first activity."

Maggie and I looked at each other. I saw in her eyes the same anxiety building in my own.

We did as we were told, getting dressed quickly. We opened the door to find a man in a white coat waiting for us, arms folded with an annoyed look on his clean-shaven face. Seeing a man's face that way was unnatural to us. He looked young, innocent and, unfortunately for him, not very intimidating.

We followed him in silence, as he lead us through the

various hallways to our destination. He handed us each a schedule to follow for the day. It had start and end times for various activities, with location information next to them. It was a very strict regimen of physical and cerebral testing. Our first stop was the cafeteria, for breakfast. We had thirty minutes to eat. We were given prepacked meal boxes, labeled with our names. We were told we didn't have to eat everything in them, but it was mandatory for us to finish the blended drink they gave us with it. They said it was full of vitamins and nutrients we needed. It was thick and grainy, unlike anything I ever had before, but it tasted good.

Next we were brought to rooms they called operatories, where we were completely wired up for monitoring for the day.

Maggie went with the flow of things. I wasn't as cooperative. We were led through a series of activities. Most were physical to start. We lifted weights, we ran and were timed. Then they tested our intelligence with logic tests, math and reading comprehension.

Everything came easy to me. I assumed Maggie would fare the same.

There were Community members in the "classes" with us, though fraternizing was frowned upon. Not that I wanted to talk to anyone anyway. I didn't recognize anyone. I got the impression they knew who Maggie and I were.

Everyone looked like I felt, confused but clean and healthy. I still felt the best I had felt in years. I was running faster, lifting more weight and finishing the tests far faster than I thought I could. Maggie was excelling too. Both of us more so than the other "subjects".

The technicians, who we started calling "Coats", because they all wore the same long, thin, white lab coat, seemed to take particular interest in us. Lots of long stares over glasses perched at the ends of noses, followed by pursed lips, furrowed brows, and nods of approval. We were lab rats, and I knew it. I was certain the rest of them knew it too, although they all took to it more like Maggie. I guess they thought it was better than sleeping out in The Elements.

"Anne." It was Dr. Kelly's voice from above.

It was the first time anyone had said my name in hours. I looked around for the camera, and found one in the corner. I raised my eyebrows as if to say, "what?". The camera moved to focus on me.

"Please take your sister, and come to my office. One of the technicians is waiting outside the classroom door to take you there."

I rolled my eyes, and walked slowly to get Maggie. She was already heading towards the door. I think it annoyed her that she wasn't spoken to directly. I loved my independent girl.

The door opened as we reached it, and a very large black man stood outside, with a distinct "don't even think of trying anything" look on his face. His name tag read "Tiny" and I chuckled. Maggie saw it too and joined in my chuckle. We both saw how unamused he was, and our eyes went to the floor as we followed him down the hall.

We passed endless unmarked doors. The hallways

looked like they were made of stainless steel. The walls, the ceiling, and floors all reflected haunting images of ourselves back to us. Our white, laceless, rubber soled shoes squeaked along as we made turn after turn down blank hallways. I tried to pay attention as best I could, but it seemed impossible. It was as if he was purposely taking us in circles to confuse us. The place was clearly designed to confuse its residents.

Maggie held my hand as we walked into Dr. Kelly's office.

"Hello, Anne. Hi, Margaret." She directed her cheerful tone to Maggie.

"I would prefer it if you called me Maggie." My strong little sister wasn't giving her an inch either.

"Okay, no problem, Maggie."

We stood completely still.

She dismissed Tiny, and sat back down behind her large metal desk, topped only with a tablet computer. I had read about them, but had never seen one in person. I didn't know the technology of it, only that it had taken the place of paper and pens and books. All the Coats carried them around, continuously tapping away. I couldn't imagine using one. This one was clear, and the date and time hovered above it in bright green. Dr. Kelly noticed me looking at it.

"Do you know what this is?" She waved her hand through the image of the date, "Are you interested in it?"

I didn't answer her.

Leaving the tablet untouched, she brought her attention back to the two of us.

"Can you please both close your eyes, and describe the room to me?"

"What? Why?" I questioned.

"Please, indulge me. Close your eyes, and describe the room."

We both did, and I squeezed Maggie's hand to signal her to go first. She understood, and spoke first.

"There are no windows, and only one door. There is a metal desk that you are sitting at, in a clear rolling chair. A metal, two drawer cabinet sits in the corner behind you. There are cameras in the right corner behind us, and the left corner behind you. The floors and walls are made of the same material as the hallways, and look like stainless steel. There is a tablet computer on the table in front of you. A speaker of some sort is in the ceiling, next to the bright white dome light above our heads. Two white folding chairs lean against the wall to the right, behind Annie. There are eight electrical outlets along the walls, with nothing plugged into them. We are standing approximately four feet, no wait, now five feet away from you, and you are wearing a white coat that covers your whole outfit, which suggests you're wearing a skirt. Your hair is red, and up in a tight bun. Your glasses are framed black, and you're lips are artificially colored mauve. You have a mole on your right cheek, and have silver metal earrings on. Annie and I are wearing white thin cotton pants and shirts, and white rubber-soled shoes without laces and are holding hands with our eyes closed. Anything to add Annie?"

I laughed, and could sense how uncomfortably

impressed Dr. Kelly was.

"Only that Dr. Kelly smells of lavender, drinks coffee with the smell of roasted nuts out of the cup that's hidden in the two drawer cabinet behind her, and she had the same sausage and eggs we had for breakfast."

With our eyes still closed, unplanned but extremely effectively we said in unison, "how did we do?"

"You can open your eyes." Dr. Kelly stood up, motioning us to the two chairs leaning against the wall. We complied, unfolding the chairs and sitting down.

Dr. Kelly breathed out slowly, looking from me then to Maggie. She tented her hands smiling.

"You two are truly extraordinary. How long have you been on your own?"

"Wait, before you start interviewing us, we have questions. Like, what the hell are we doing here?" I didn't care for the compliment, I wanted answers.

"Okay, that's fair." She placed her tented hands to her chin, and continued. "You and your sister, along with the others you've seen here, are all part of a very important project. The Savior Project. You have all survived for quite some time out in The Elements. You have all honed some very important and impressive skills, without formal training or teachings. Skills that have helped you successfully navigate and survive out in The Elements.

"The earth has changed, as you know, and it is going to continue to evolve. The nearly barren lands are running out of resources. Our climate controlled Estates are going to start to fail. We need to figure out a way to survive when that happens."

"So you're studying us, to see how we do it?" Maggie asked, her eyes wide and confused.

"Yes, Maggie."

"But that's not all you want from us." I said, not believing it was that simple.

"Well, no." Dr. Kelly sat back in her chair before continuing.

"Your bodies have evolved to adapt to your environment as well, and when taken care of properly, will be capable of extraordinary things. I'm sure you've noticed a change in yourselves already."

It was true. I felt stronger, faster, smarter.

"We intend to study you, and see what it is that has happened, to you and your sister in particular."

"Why us? Why are we so special?"

"Well, first of all, you were born after the earth changed. Your parents had already spent quite some time evolving and adapting to The Elements. You're very special you see. You're a First Gen, the first generation born out in The Elements."

Chapter Nine

Before Maggie and I had a chance to ask any more questions, the doors opened, and two Coats whisked us away to separate operatories. I resisted, as I always did, giving them a hard time just to spite them. They hooked me up to various machines, and gave me a shot of something that made me very sleepy. Unable to stand, I sat down on the operatory bed. It had different settings, so you could sit when it was in the upright position, or lay down when it was flat. I tried desperately to stay awake, watching them preparing a clear plastic bag of fluid, and hanging it on a pole next to me. I mumbled some words, trying to ask what they were giving me, but it was unintelligible even to me.

They placed the bed in the flat position, and laid me down. I didn't have any control over my body. Everything went hazy, then blue. Everywhere I turned looked like it had a blue gauzy film over it. My hearing was muffled, invisible ear muffs blocking any sound.

My whole body felt heavy. I could barely lift my arm. There was commotion around me. I couldn't really make out what was happening. A lot of shouting and movement. My head felt hot, my breathing short and labored. I felt a hand on my forehead, then more commotion.

Were they trying to revive me? Was I dying? I started to focus on steadying my breathing and heart rate.

I could hear more clearly, and Dr. Kelly's voice rang above everyone else.

"What the hell are you trying to do? Kill her? Get out, all of you, get out!"

The blue haze seemed to lift and I saw all the Coats scatter.

"Anne, Anne! Can you hear me?"

I wanted to speak but couldn't. I nodded.

She looked relieved. She placed a soft plastic mask over my face. A blast of cold air filled my mouth and nose. My forehead was drenched with sweat, but I felt cold. My body started to tremble. It was a feeling I was familiar with. I was going into shock. I flashed back to the time it happened; to a woman in our old Pride who had broken her leg. Uncle Joe explained to me what was happening to her. I remembered being so scared for her.

I felt heavy blankets fall on top of me. The trembling was uncontrollable. When this had happened in the past, Maggie and I would sit dangerously close to the fire and hold each other tight. I needed my sister.

What on earth had they given me? I wanted to ask Dr. Kelly a lot of questions, but I still couldn't speak.

"Anne, we are going to regulate your temperature, and get you feeling a lot better right away."

She sounded genuine, less mechanical than she had previously. All I could do was nod.

I felt her inject something through the needle in my arm. It was cold and stung slightly. I felt like I was floating then everything went black.

When I woke up again, I felt rejuvenated and really awake. I didn't have that groggy feeling I was used to upon first waking up. I knew where I was right away. I could hear better. All of the sounds around me, I recognized in an instant. I made a quick mental list of my surroundings, then closed my eyes and it was a photograph in my mind. I could give a complete description. I magically knew the square footage of the room; how many tiles were in the ceiling. I could smell and recognize the scents around me. I could tell that Dr. Kelly and her lavender cream had recently been in the room, and that someone else who had been in there had eaten something with garlic. The sounds were almost unbearable though. So very loud. I could almost hear the blood pump through my veins. It was reminiscent of the descriptions given to a newly turned vampire in the books I found and read. I knew that wasn't what was happening to me. I wanted to see Maggie, talk to her, find out if she was going through the same changes, the same enhancements. That's what they were. What they felt like.

Enhancements.

Chapter Ten

"Annie?" Maggie appeared at my door.

I jumped up, running to her and wrapped my arms around her.

"Mags, are you okay?"

"I'm fine, I'm great. I feel better than I have ever felt."

"Me too," I whispered, aware of the eyes and ears behind the cameras in the room.

"What are they doing to us? I'm scared."

Finally, I thought to myself. She's realizing that this isn't a good thing what they're doing.

"Anne," Dr. Kelly's voice came from the speaker in the ceiling. We both looked up then to the camera in the corner.

"It's time for your training."

"Training for what? What are we training for?"

"Today you are being assessed in your fighting skills."

This was actually appealing to both of us. A chance to kick the crap out of the people holding us here.

"Okay, where do you want us?" I winked at Maggie

and she smiled.

"Do we get to fight together?"

"Yes, Maggie, at first. I will meet you both in the gym."

Tiny appeared behind Maggie, stone faced as usual. We followed him down the maze of corridors to the gym.

Standing with Dr. Kelly were seven men and two women, all dressed for a work out. They didn't look like other Community members. I was glad. I didn't want to fight against any of our own. Another door opened, and a boy dressed like us walked in. I didn't recognize him from any of the Prides we knew, but he was clearly there for the same reason we were. I wondered if we would fight against him or with him. My curiosity was answered quickly, as Dr. Kelly motioned for him to stand with us. Three community members versus nine Staties. This was going to be a cakewalk.

The Staties got together in a huddle. The three of us stood at the ready.

"Malakai." He nodded towards me.

"Anne. That's Maggie, my sister."

"Nice to meet you." He smiled then got back into a ready stance.

Dr. Kelly moved to the sidelines.

The nine Staties leapt out of their huddle, and at us. We were ready.

The two women went after Maggie, three men came at me and four men went at Malakai.

I didn't see how she did it, but Maggie was through with the two women faster than I could get rid of one of my attackers. She joined to helped me. Backs to each other, we dispatched the other men swiftly, and went to help Malakai who needed little aid. The fight lasted about four minutes.

We stood barely sweating or breathing heavy, while our nine assailants lay crumpled on the floor, bloody and exhausted.

"Really?" Malakai asked looking at Dr. Kelly. "Please tell me that's not the best you got. That wasn't even a warm up."

"Okay, Malakai. You three have proven that fighting is a skill that you have mastered more so than the Colonists who live here."

"That's not it, though," I interjected.

"What do you mean, Anne?"

"Maggie and I are fast and strong, and know how to fight, but I've never been this fast or strong. What are you giving us?"

"Like I've already told you, we're taking care of you. Better than you were ever able to take care of yourselves out in The Elements. Your morning protein shakes contain the nutrients and vitamins you need."

"So that whole thing yesterday, when you freaked about the other Coats trying to kill me?"

Dr. Kelly shifted. She averted her eyes. She didn't know I was awake and aware during all of it.

"One of the Coats, as you call them, pushed a little too much adrenaline into your IV line."

"Oh great, good to know we have a bunch of geniuses caring for us in here." Malakai moved closer to me and Maggie, I guessed as a sign of solidarity.

"Okay, that's enough. You can go back to your rooms until it's time to eat."

Tiny was suddenly behind us.

"Hey, Tiny, you would certainly have lasted longer than these chumps." Malakai teased the big man attempting, without success, to make him smile. Maggie giggled.

Without a word, Tiny escorted all three of us back to our rooms. We got to our room first.

"It was a pleasure kicking butt with you guys."

"Bye, Malakai!" Maggie shouted, cheerfully waving as Tiny hurried him around the corner.

"You can call me Kai!" he shouted over his shoulder, as he went out of sight.

I just smiled.

"He's funny," Maggie added, as she skipped off into her room.

I was curious about him. Was he a first gen like us? He was about my age; it would make sense. I hoped we would encounter him again.

Chapter Eleven

The days to follow were exhausting. Much to our disappointment, we didn't get to fight again, and we didn't see Malakai again. It was strange. It was almost as if they were keeping us apart. Maggie and I barely saw each other. By the time we got back to our room, we were both too tired to talk about our days. Most of the time we didn't even say goodnight, simply collapsing in our respective beds, and sleeping soundly until morning.

This particular evening, I had just fallen asleep, when I heard a knock at my door. My bedroom door. Maggie would usually just let herself in and climb into my bed.

"Hey, Anne, are you awake?"

It was Malakai. I couldn't imagine how he got into our suite. I hurried to the door, and opened it enough to see him.

"How did you get in here?"

"Tiny. I hope it's okay."

I opened the door further.

"Really?"

"He's actually pretty cool once you get him talking. Apparently he doesn't really like Dr. Kelly and the rest of the Coats. His real name is Luther Tyson."

"Tyson, as in Calvin Tyson?"

"Yup, he's a nephew or cousin or something."

"How can you be here right now? Aren't they watching?" I pointed at the cameras.

"Tiny took care of that too. Come on out."

We stepped out into the living area, and sat on the couch. It was strange having anyone else in our space. It was dark, and painfully quiet. Every movement made a sound. Our whispering was so loud, I felt like the whole Combine would hear us.

He sat next to me. As my eyes got used to the darkness, I could see his face clearer. He was slightly out of breath, and smiling.

"How did you get Tiny to do all this for you?"

He went on to tell me how one night, when Tiny was escorting him back to his room, he just starting talking to him completely out of the blue. He told him all about what we were doing there, and why. How he didn't agree with the way they were treating the people they brought in from The Community. They called us Commons, they thought we were savages, uncivilized, uneducated. They didn't know how smart we really had to be to survive out there, until they started kidnapping us, and bringing us in here to study. The studies had started about a year before we were picked up. They sent people out into The Community to set up cameras to observe us. They took interest in certain Prides, and then specific people. They followed them to see how they lived, how they survived. They took particular interest in kids like us. First Gens. Malakai's parents also met and had him after The Shift. They also died a while ago. Malakai joined another Pride, and our paths had never crossed. I was riveted to his story, hanging on every word.

"I always wanted to meet you two."

"What? What do you mean?"

"You guys are legend in The Community."

"What? No. You're joking."

"Seriously, you and Maggie are known throughout The Community, and with The Staties. They've been studying you guys for a while. The fact that you've been out on your own as long as you have, not joining another Pride, taking care of your sister, teaching her. It's pretty remarkable."

I looked away from him, embarrassed and confused. I never thought of what me and Maggie did as anything but survival.

"Don't be embarrassed, it's incredibly cool. It was awesome fighting next to you two the other day. I'm not surprised they haven't asked us to do that again. It was a total beat down. I bet they're still recovering."
He laughed.

My face was warm as I watched him looking at me, as if I was some kind of hero. I needed to get the focus off myself.

"You're not a bad fighter yourself, Kai."

"Those guys were pathetic."

I studied his features. He was handsome, blue eyes

sparkling through the dim light of the sitting room. A flash of dark hair, that looked deliberately tousled. He was smiling, and looked relaxed, at ease with our situation. I was jealous. I still felt on edge, tense, all the time. This was an exceptionally awkward situation for me.

"How long have you been here?"

"They grabbed me about three weeks before they got you and Maggie."

We talked for a little while longer. He told me the fight he put up when they took him. He had been scouting for a pull same as I was. His Pride was behind him, waiting for him to signal. He wasn't sure what happened to them afterward.

My eyes were getting heavy. Malakai yawned. As if he'd been watching, Tiny appeared at my door.

"I guess that's my cue. Gotta go, it was a pleasure Anne."

"You can call me Annie."

"See you soon, Annie. Tell Maggie I say hi."

I smiled and nodded at Tiny, who didn't say a word

and they left.

I sat there for a while, taking in everything that Malakai told me. It was all so unbelievable. It was crazy to think anyone admired me. Who was I? I was nobody. Just a simple Common to these people who held us captive. It was hard to believe Malakai was ever caught after seeing him fight. I hated to think it, but I was glad they were able to get him. I was thankful to have someone my own age to talk to. I didn't know how many chances we would get to talk like that. I was tired, but sad he had to go. My head filled with images of the things Malakai told me. I checked on Maggie, who was sleeping soundly. I decided I needed to do the same.

Chapter Twelve

The next morning, I found myself anxious to find Malakai. Maggie and I were escorted to the cafeteria by someone other than Tiny. I hoped he hadn't gotten in trouble for helping Malakai.

"Hey Annie, there's Kai!" Maggie was waving emphatically at him.

I felt my stomach flutter, and my face flush. I looked up, and he was heading towards our table. I sat up straighter, and wondered if he would notice that I had done my hair different, or the lip gloss that I put on.

He placed his tray on our table and whispered in my ear. "Did you sleep alright?"

I just nodded, unable to speak. I had never experienced these feelings before. There was never an opportunity to. I was annoyed at myself, not used to being around boys I wasn't trying to beat up. It was all so new to me.

We ate and made small talk, as we drank our shakes. Maggie dominated the conversation with questions for Kai. He was very patient with her, and I appreciated it.

Breakfast was over too quickly, and it was time to get wired up for tracking for the day. Three Coats came to our table, and we were escorted separately to our operatories.

I was so used to the process I could have placed all the sensors onto myself. But I let the young Coat fumble through it on his own. He was particularly clumsy. His name was Hutch Alexander, at least according to his name tag. I wasn't sure if Hutch was his first name or last name. Last names confounded me. I guess the Pride names could be our last names, if we really want to have one. Hutch, or Alexander, seemed really nervous.

"First day?" I asked, half kidding.

"I'm sorry, is it that obvious?"

"No, no, just relax. Here," I took the sensors from him and placed them on my head and neck, like the other Coats had done to me before.

"What should I call you?"

"Hutch is fine."

"Is that your first name? Your name tag is confusing."

"Huh? Oh, yeah, Hutch is my first name. Alexander is my last name."

"I don't have a last name." I lifted my shirt, and placed more censors on my chest. Hutch turned away, which I thought was polite, and unlike any of the other Coats.

"Okay, I'm all set."

"Thanks for doing that, I appreciate it."

"No problem. Don't worry, you'll get it."

He led me back to the gym, where they were testing agility again. I went through a series of timed obstacle courses. There were about seven other community members being tested with me, none of whom were Kai or Maggie.

I went through the session without resistance or argument, much to the surprise and relief of the Coats administering the testing. I felt bad for my new handler, Hutch, and wanted him to look good on his first day. He stayed for the whole session, furiously punching notes into his tablet.

He didn't look much older than me and Kai.

He was awkward and funny. Only about an inch taller than me, medium build, dirty blonde hair. A very chiseled jaw, and a nice smile that lit up his whole face the rare moments he let one escape.

"Are you going to be my new shadow?" I asked.

His being so awkward and nervous somehow made me feel confident and strong.

"Yes, Anne. I've been assigned to you."

"You can call me Annie."

"That's okay. We're not friends Anne, you are my subject."

The way he said it sounded rehearsed, and it actually made me laugh instead of being insulting.

"Yes sir, not friends." I saluted mockingly.

"I mean; those are the rules. I'm not allowed to become emotionally attached to who I am assigned to."

I laughed again and followed him back to the operatory. I hopped up onto the gurney, and he carefully removed the sensors from me, hands shaking. Poor thing. He gets me as his first assignment.

"I'll get better at this, I promise."

"Don't worry about it."

I smiled at him. He looked up and smiled back at me. He seemed to relax a little.

He escorted me back to my room. Maggie was there.

"Do you want to come in, and see how the other half lives?"

"I should get back."

"Really quick, just come meet my sister."

He followed me in, hesitantly. Maggie looked up, suspicious.

"Maggie, this is Hutch. He's my new handler."

"Hi, I got a new one today too. Cindy. She's cool."

"Nice to meet you, Maggie." Hutch smiled, and extended his hand. Maggie shook it enthusiastically, his smile melting her suspicions away.

"Okay, well, I should go. See you tomorrow, Anne."

And he disappeared out the door.

"He's cute," Maggie said, getting back to the puzzle she was working on.

I just smiled, and got ready for dinner.

They encouraged us to dress up for dinner. Unlike breakfast and lunch, dinner was set up like a sit down restaurant, where we sat and ordered from menus, and got served by a wait staff. Until that day, I didn't bother. Now, I felt like I wanted to dress nice, in case we saw Kai. Maggie liked wearing the nice clothes they provided. She came running into my room, clad in one of her many dresses, and plopped down unceremoniously onto my bed.

"You look pretty. Why?"

"Gee, thanks kid."

"You know what I mean. You never dress up for dinner. Why now?"

"I don't know, I just felt like it. Can't let these perfect good dresses go to waste. C'mon, let's go."

We rang for an escort to take us to dinner. I was getting better, but we still didn't know our way around The Combine. To our surprise, Hutch showed up.

"Oh. hello. Didn't think you would be escorting us."

"Hi. You look beautiful." He said it without thinking, I could tell he regretted saying it as soon as the words escaped his lips.

"Thanks. You look nice, too."

He had gotten dressed for dinner, too. He wore a black tailored jacket, with a white button down shirt, a blue tie, and black pants. He looked very handsome and smelled very clean.

"I'm sorry, that was incredibly inappropriate."

"What's inappropriate about telling a girl she's beautiful?" Maggie called over her shoulder, as she ran ahead of us.

I smiled, and could feel my face redden. It had been the reaction I was looking for when I got ready that evening, but not from Hutch. Not that I minded.

We walked in silence. Maggie was far ahead of us, and I called for her to hang back. She was proving to have a better sense of where she was going than I did.

"C'mon, don't you want to get a table with Kai?"

"Kai?" Hutch looked at me curious.

"Malakai, he's from The Community like us. He's around our age."

"Oh, yes, I know who he is. He is very strong and fast."

When we got to the cafeteria, Maggie spotted Kai and bee-lined to his table.

"Do you want to come sit with us?"

"No, thank you. It's probably not a good idea."

I understood why, so I didn't press him. He seemed sad, and I felt bad for him as he went to sit at a table by himself.

Kai stood when I got to the table.

"I hear it's what a gentleman is supposed to do when a lady joins him at the table."

He pulled my chair out, and I sat down.

"You're like the prince and Annie is the princess," Maggie giggled, enjoying the scene.

I felt ridiculous, and I felt like everyone was watching us. I scanned the room, and my eyes locked with Hutch's, who was watching us.

He turned away, realizing I had seen him staring.

"Ready to eat?" Kai handed me a menu.

"Yes, I'm starving."

Dinner was the most enjoyable I had ever had. Our conversation was easy. We actually laughed, a lot. People were watching us enjoying ourselves. I didn't care anymore. The food seemed to taste better. We ordered dessert for the first time. Maggie and I regretting not having gotten it before. Chocolate Mousse, they called it. I was always terrified to order it before, picturing some kind of animal, not the silky smooth deliciousness it turned out to be. We lingered long after the food was gone. I looked up, and noticed Hutch was still there. He looked away whenever I glanced his way. When we finally left, I waved to him. He smiled, and waved back. He had sat alone the whole time.

Tiny met us at the exit of the cafeteria, and escorted us back to our rooms. They were called Domiciles by the Colonists and Coats who lived in The Combine.

"Hey. Tiny, any chance we can get another favor soon?"

Tiny didn't even look at Kai. I didn't know what that meant. As far as I was concerned, Tiny was a mute. He never spoke around me and Maggie.

"Maybe I'll see you later," Kai whispered to me when we got to our door. I could feel his breath on my ear, and it made my stomach flutter. I just smiled, unable to speak.

"Goodnight, Maggie!"

"Bye Kai, see you at breakfast!" Maggie ran to her room, kicking off her dressy shoes on the way in, and shutting her bedroom door behind her.

I sat on the couch in the living room, thinking about our dinner with Kai. It was the most fun I'd had, ever. It felt like a life, a real life. One I never thought I would ever experience. I thought about what the girl wrote about in the journal we shared. Some of the things she wrote started to make sense to me. Then my thoughts went to Hutch, sitting alone the entire time watching us having a wonderful time. I felt guilty. He had looked so sad.

I got ready for bed, and much to my surprise, after

having such an amazing time with Kai, fell asleep thinking about Hutch.

Chapter Thirteen

The next morning, when Maggie and I called for an escort to breakfast, Hutch showed up again.

"Stuck with us again?"

"I wouldn't call it stuck. I was on my way to the cafeteria for breakfast too, so I thought since I pass right by your Domicile every morning, it made sense."

"You pass here every morning?" Maggie ran to his side, interested in him.

"Yes. My Domicile isn't far from yours."

"Really? You live here too? What's yours like?"

"Maggie, leave him alone."

"No, it's okay. Mine isn't nearly as nice as yours."

He patted her on the back reassuringly. I was suddenly curious about him. I hadn't really thought about where the Coats all lived. I figured this was a job they came to everyday, and then went home to their families at night.

Out in The Community, we didn't have jobs we were paid to do. There were no bosses or employees like I read about or we were told about. Our lives, though only separated by Plexiglas, were worlds apart. I didn't believe studying us would ever give them any more understanding of how very differently we lived. That wasn't why they were studying us anyway. They needed us to save themselves. The Savior Project.

When we got to the cafeteria, Kai wasn't there. Maggie invited Hutch to eat with us, and he accepted this time.

"Not inappropriate for breakfast, then?"

"It doesn't feel to be. I am your handler, so it makes sense for us to eat, then go straight into your schedule for the day."

"Okay, if that's what you need to tell yourself." I teased. I found him easy to be around.

"I can go eat somewhere else, if you'd like."

"Don't you dare!" Maggie ordered, grabbing his hand. "There's no way we're letting you sit alone again, like you did last night."

We all laughed, then got in line for our meal boxes. My shake had changed considerably since the first one I had. This time it was a completely different color. It tasted even better. Maggie's hadn't changed. Hutch didn't have one to drink. Maggie offered to let him taste hers. He declined, saying she needed to finish the whole thing.

We ate, and laughed, as we had with Kai the night before. We drew some looks, mostly from the Coats this time. They seemed to disapprove of Hutch eating with us. Hutch was completely oblivious to them. He looked to be enjoying himself like he hadn't before in his life. He beamed listening to Maggie and I tell stories about our life outside the bubble. He was truly fascinated, and interested in our experiences.

Then it was time to start our day. Cindy, Maggie's handler, came up to our table to collect Maggie. Hutch and I went together to Op 8.

"You wanna try it this time?" I asked him, pointing at the sensors.

"Sure, okay."

He did better, and was very proud of himself.

"See, I told you it would get easier."

"Thank you, Anne."

"So, you how long have you lived here in the lab?"

"My whole life."

I looked up, in shock and surprise.

"Your whole life?"

"Yes."

"Do you have any siblings?"

"No. If I did, I would hope to be close like you and Maggie. What you have is really special."

"What?"

"Nothing. Never mind, let's get started."

"What about your parents?"

"My father is here. My mother died a long time ago."

"Oh, sorry." I felt my face redden.

"Yeah, well, why don't we just get started." Hutch shifted uncomfortably.

"Okay. Sorry, Hutch, I didn't know."

"How would you know? Just forget it. Let's go, we're already late."

He was agitated. I complied and dropped the subject.

We spent the rest of the day basically in silence, only interacting when we had to.

At lunch, Maggie and I ate with Kai. Hutch disappeared, and returned to trials after.

I really hated the awkwardness. It made me uncomfortable and unreasonably angry.

"Are we done?" I asked, with all the frustration from the day clear in my voice.

Hutch looked up, surprised by my tone. I was equally surprised.

"Can you hurry it up? I have to get ready for dinner."

I wasn't sure why I was being so mean.

"Yes, of course. Sorry."

He fumbled with the wires.

"Here, let me." I ripped the sensors off and jumped off the table.

"Anne, what's wrong?"

"Nothing. Do I have to wait for you to escort me

back?" I was making for the door. The feeling of frustration and anger was overwhelming.

"I'll just be a moment." He was confused, and I couldn't blame him. I wasn't being reasonable.

I huffed and paced the room until he was ready.

"Finally," I said exasperated. I had no idea why I was acting this way.

We walked back to my Domicile in silence. Before I could escape inside, Hutch spoke.

"Anne, I'm sorry you're upset. I don't like to talk about myself. I've been trained not to. They don't want us to get close to you guys. They are afraid it will influence the study. If I tell you about me, confide in you, and you confide in me, if we become friends, they are afraid I will keep information from them."

"I understand. I'm sorry for being such a jerk. My emotions have been all over the place lately." My tone was soft and regretful.

"So, see you tomorrow?" He asked his voice hopeful.

"Yes, bright and early." I smiled and opened my door.

He stood there while my door slid closed between us.

Chapter Fourteen

Each morning, Hutch would meet us to escort us to breakfast. We did become friends, despite the rules Hutch was so worried about following. Maggie had met another little First Gen girl named Abby. She was cute, long dark brown hair like mine, brown eyes like Maggie. She came with the last new recruit drop.

Newbies, as they were known, came in every six weeks. I didn't get to know any of the other Community members besides Kai. I had no interest. There were definitely more recruits than there were subjects. I wasn't sure where they put everyone. I only counted about thirty of us at a time.

Abby and Maggie started eating together and playing together. I liked seeing her happy, and having fun. Though I was seeing less of her, and I didn't like that so much. She told me Abby's parents had died when she was three, and she stayed with her Pride. She had an older brother, Kyle, who wasn't brought in. She didn't know where he was. He didn't stay with their

Pride after their parents were gone. There were only two other Newbies brought in with her. I only saw her. I don't know what happened to the others.

I asked Hutch one day what happened to The Community members we didn't see anymore. He said he didn't know. I wasn't sure if he did and didn't want to tell me, or truly didn't know. I dropped it, not really wanting to know.

Hutch and I were building an odd friendship, based on curiosity and questions. Once he threw the regulations out the window, he wanted to know everything about living out in The Elements. He listened intently, while Maggie and I chattered on about our lives growing up. Our normalcy fascinated him.

Kai stopped coming to breakfast. He said he liked to sleep in anytime he got the chance. Whatever they were putting in his current shake gave him spurts of energy, and then he'd crash hard, and all he'd want to do was sleep. We only got the shakes at breakfast, so he skipped as often as he could. Nobody seemed to care, according to him. I didn't know we had the option. We saw him at lunch and dinner. It worked. I liked having breakfast with Hutch.

"So you grew up a Statie?"

"Is that what you guys call us? I thought I was just a Coat to you."

"Well, not everyone who lives in these bubbles wear lab coats. You live in these big estates. I guess that's where the nickname came from. What do you call yourselves?"

"Colonists."

"And you call us Commons. Not exactly a flattering term."

"No, I suppose not. I never really thought about it, just as you never really thought about why you call us Staties."

"Is it weird for you, talking to me? As weird as it is for me, talking to you?"

He smiled, not answering my question.

"My dad is a researcher; I grew up in these labs, helping him. This is really all I've ever known."

"How long have you been testing 'my kind'?"

"Honestly, I don't ever remember not testing The Commons, in one way or another."

"And do you think it's okay, what you do? Plucking people away from their homes, so you can treat them like lab rats?" I was suddenly angry.

"I never really thought of it that way. I always thought of it as rescuing."

"Rescuing? Rescuing us from what?" My anger was growing. I couldn't believe how righteous he sounded. Hutch didn't seem to notice how upset I was.

"The Elements. It's bad out there Anne. The air you're breathing; the water you drink. You're pulling food out of the garbage. Do you think that's safe?"

"At least we're free."

"Free from what? To die a slow, painful death? I, for one, don't want that for you."

"What do you mean?"

"You deserve better, Anne."

He looked sincere. I calmed down, realizing he genuinely thought he was doing good.

"Have you ever been out there?"

"No."

"Do you ever want to go out there?"

"I have wanted to my whole life. Father always forbade it."

"Hutch, you're not a kid anymore. You can do whatever you want."

"I wish that were true. As soon as I turned eighteen, father assigned me to The Savior Project. That was about six months ago. Now that I'm working in The Combine, we can't risk contamination, I was born in here. I'm a First Gen Colonist."

"So, are they studying you too?"

"I've been studied my whole life."

It made me look at him differently, knowing he understood a bit of what I was going through. I thought about what it must have been like, having a researcher for a father. Always being looked at as a specimen to study.

"I'm sorry." I said, looking at him.

"For what?" he asked, not looking at me.

"That you had to grow up like that."

"Oh, it's not so bad. I've had an okay life. Just a bit sheltered. Father would never let me do much of what the other kids were allowed to do, because he considered me very important. There aren't that many of us. The Estates put limits on how many children families could have. They didn't want to risk overpopulation."

I thought that was smart, and wished my parents had had the same rule.

"Most of the other First Gen Colonists live pretty lavish lives in other Estates. They don't know how important they are, and they spend most of their time being pretty self-destructive. I never really had anything in common with them."

"So, what do you do for fun in here?"

"Fun?"

"Do you have any friends to hang out with?"

"No."

"A girlfriend?"

"No. Never."

He looked almost embarrassed, or maybe just sad.

"So, do you ever leave here?"

"No, I'm here all the time. Living in The Combine makes things easier."

"What is your place like?"

He avoided my question,

"I helped design yours." He proclaimed it proudly.

"Really?"

"Yes. It took months to create a place that you and your sister would be comfortable in, based on what we knew about you."

I frowned. I didn't like that he knew me because they'd been studying me for months. I hated thinking about what video footage they had of me. Who knew what they saw us doing.

He noticed my frown, and spoke.

"Anne, I only read about you. They gave me a file of you and Maggie to base my design on. I didn't watch any of the video footage they had. I only had pictures. One of Maggie, and one of you."

"Can I see your place?"

"I don't know. I don't think that would be a good

idea."

"What? Why? You've seen ours."

"Yes, but that probably wasn't a good idea either."

"Why? Because you're not supposed to get emotionally attached to your subjects?"

I was mocking him.

"That's exactly why."

"Don't you consider me a friend?"

"I---"

"Well, I consider you my friend. So, even if you don't want to get emotionally attached to me, you can't control how I feel about you."

He looked up at me, and smiled.

"Okay, after trials, I will show you my place."

We finished breakfast, and went to Op 8 to get wired up. Hutch had improved greatly, and we got through the hook up quicker each day.

I went through my different exercises, and he punched things into his tablet. It was different than it had been before. It was almost fun.

We broke for lunch, and Hutch said he was meeting

116

his father; they were eating together. I was surprised to find myself disappointed.

He brought me to the cafeteria, where Maggie and Kai were waiting for me.

"See you after," he whispered.

"Okay, bye." I whispered back.

"Annie! Come sit!" Maggie waved to me to join her and Kai.

"How was your morning, kid?"

"It was fine. Cindy had me doing more stuff today than normal."

"Yeah?"

"My handler had me doing different stuff today too. How's your handler, Annie?" Kai's tone was strange.

"He's fine."

"You guys seem pretty friendly."

"Well, it's hard not to be when you spend your whole day with them."

I felt the need to defend myself and Hutch.

"I spend all day with my handler, and I don't even know his name."

"Really? You're joking." Maggie spoke through a mouthful of bran muffin.

"Nope. We could seriously care less about each other. In fact, I hate him, and everything he stands for."

"They're just doing their job, Kai."

"Right." He said it sarcastically.

"So, tell me Mags, what new stuff did Cindy have you do?"

Maggie took the opening, and gave us a full detailed report of her morning session with Cindy. I only heard part of it.

Looking around, I could see other Community members, and the lives they were making for themselves there. They chatted with each other, built friendships. I thought maybe some of them were forming relationships. Romantic ones. I wondered what it would be like to hold someone's hand, other than my sister's. I don't think I could have survived without having Maggie to hug, and hold, and cuddle with. She always believed she needed me more than I needed her, but the truth was she was my motivation, my life's driving force.

My mind went to Hutch. Did he have anyone like that? What must it be like to not have anyone to hold, or touch? A hug, a hand to hold, when you're scared. He must be so lonely. I found myself crying for him.

"Annie, what's wrong?"

"Nothing, I was just thinking about something. I'm fine. We should clean up, and get ready for the afternoon session."

"Will I see you at dinner?" Kai asked hopeful.

"Yes, of course." I answered.

"What about later?"

"Later, when?" I was confused.

"Tiny said he might be able to swing a visit again."

"Oh, okay."

"Unless you don't want me to."

"No, of course I do. Dinner and then later too."

We cleaned up, and I went to the bathroom to throw water on my face. I felt so silly for crying in front of them. My emotions were truly unpredictable lately.

I met Hutch back in our Op.

"What's wrong?" He asked, concern in his voice.

I smiled at him.

"Are you okay?"

I didn't say anything. I got up from the bed, and hugged him.

He didn't hug me back. He stood there awkwardly.

"Anne, what are you doing?"

"I thought you might need one."

I let go, and stepped back.

"Okay." He stared at me, confused. "Thank you?"

"You're welcome."

I didn't know how he felt, but I felt better.

We went through the afternoon session, and after we detached all my sensors, we left.

We journeyed down the metal halls. The walk seemed longer than any had before it. I was excited to finally see where Hutch lived. He said his Domicile was like ours, but I didn't believe him. I thought it would be nicer, more like a home.

I was wrong. It was very plain, much plainer than ours. It looked very sterile, boring. It amazed me that he had designed ours.

He was nervous to show me his place. I didn't know why. He showed me the living room and the kitchen. His kitchen was much nicer than ours, I guess because he didn't always want his meals served to him. He even showed me his bathroom, which was spotless. His place was unexpectedly neat.

"What about your bedroom?" I asked, curious to see all of it.

"What about it?" He asked, shifting uncomfortably.

"I want to see it."

"It's not any different than yours, really. Besides it's a mess."

"Oh come on, your place is completely different than ours. Please?"

He reluctantly led me to his room, and the door slid open. It wasn't anything spectacular, and it wasn't messy like he had said. I didn't understand right away why he didn't want me to see it. Then I noticed it hanging on his wall. Two pictures of me. One from before I was in The Combine, all bundled up in my multiple layers of tattered clothes. I had my ear flap hat on, and a thick scarf around my neck but you could see my whole dirt-covered face. I had no clue when it was taken. The other was of me sitting in Op 8. It looked like what I remembered as being the first day I woke up after being captured. I was dressed in my Combine uniform, my hair still wet.

I looked at Hutch. His eyes were to the floor. I didn't understand why he had them pinned to his wall. He said he had pictures of me and Maggie, but not that he had it as the only art on his walls. I didn't know whether to feel embarrassed or angry.

"Why are they hanging on your wall?"

He looked up, his face red with embarrassment.

"I was assigned to your case months before you were brought here. They gave me information on you and Maggie."

"So you *have* been watching me?" I was mortified.

"They didn't have any cameras set up anywhere inappropriate. And I only saw some of what they had. I saw you fight, train and teach Maggie, loot from The

Estates. The way you set up, and made for The Estates when you needed things. Your campsite, how you lived. You are truly amazing. I admired you so much, for your strength and drive."

"You admired me?"

"You and Maggie. You're both amazing." Hutch was embarrassed, I could tell. I had a lump in my throat. I didn't know how to feel.

"I don't know what to say." I finally spoke.

"I'm sorry I lied. I didn't want you to feel self-conscious."

He paused, and started to shake his head.

"This is bad; you shouldn't be here." He started to shuffle me out of his room.

"Why, because your father wouldn't approve?"

"No, because I'm not supposed to know you. You're definitely not supposed to know me. I'm not supposed to *want* to know you. You are my assignment, not my friend."

I was hurt. The way he said it was mean and dismissive.

"Fine. Take me back to my room."

We didn't say anything after that. He walked me back to my room. I could tell he wanted to say something to me, but I wouldn't look at him to give him the chance to say anything.

When we got back to my Domicile, I quickly went in, without looking at him.

He grabbed my arm gently, to stop me.

"Anne, I'm sorry. I'm sorry for what I said, and how I said it."

"It's fine. Like you said, we're not friends. It doesn't matter."

"Please don't be like that."

"I have to go, I'm meeting Maggie and Kai for dinner."

"Okay, I'll see you tomorrow."

He stood there, looking sad as the door slid closed on him. I put my hands on the cool metal of it. I pictured him, still standing on the other side of it.

It wasn't his fault. My life had changed so much. I looked around at what we called our home now, and I missed our campsite. The life we knew before. Mine and Maggie's. It was harder, and simpler at the same time. I had emotions running through me that I had never experienced before. I cared about Hutch. I wanted him to be happy. I wanted to be his friend.

I barely spoke through dinner. Kai and Maggie talked about their afternoons, and didn't seem to notice my silence.

Maggie wanted to hang out with Abby after dinner, which left me alone again.

I knew Kai would be stopping by later that night, so I thought I would lay down, and maybe nap. When I got back to my room, there was a single white rose on my bed, with a note.

Anne, I am so sorry for this afternoon. Please forgive me.

It was from Hutch. I put the rose to my nose, and breathed in the sweet smell of it. Tapped it to my lips. The soft petals felt like suede. I had never seen one in person. It was beautiful. I laid down on my bed, holding it to my cheek so I could feel its coolness brush my skin. I wished I could go find him, and talk to him, and tell him it was okay. Instead, I fell asleep.

I woke up to Maggie plopping onto my bed.

"Nice flower. Where'd you get it?"

"It was here when I got back after dinner."

"Kai?"

"No, Hutch."

"Really?" Her eyes were wide with surprise and curiosity.

"Yeah, we had a little disagreement earlier, and he wanted to apologize."

"Where can you even get a rose? I've never seen a real one." She picked it up and studied it, smelling it, feeling the petals.

I thought about that for a moment. I didn't know. He would have had to have left The Combine.

She left my room, yawning and saying goodnight. She seemed to be growing up faster, being in there. Socializing with others would definitely lead to that. She was like a little sponge, absorbing all the information we were given, excelling daily at her trials. They were all impressed with her, and had long stopped giving me credit for it. She was special, and they knew it now too. I was very proud of her.

At the same time, I felt I was losing her. She didn't need me anymore. She had her own things, other things that didn't have anything to do with me. I wasn't as important to her anymore. It made me sad.

A lot of what was happening did. I didn't have control over anything anymore. I went from dictating how Maggie and I lived to having all of my freedom stripped away. My surroundings unfamiliar. Needing to navigate my way around people. All of a sudden caring about what strangers thought of me. Feeling emotions I never had before. It was too much.

Malakai knocked late that night. I almost didn't want to see him. I wanted to see Hutch. Tell him I forgive him. Kai was strong, and didn't need anyone. He made friends, and could take care of himself. He didn't need me, either.

Hutch did. Hutch needed me to forgive him.

Kai could tell something was wrong.

"What's going on with you? Is everything alright?" He sounded sincere, genuinely concerned.

"Yeah, I'm fine. Just tired. I've been feeling wiped out lately."

"They work you too hard. They're the hardest on you."

"I don't think so. I think you're working just as hard, or even harder than I do."

"No, they work you non-stop throughout the day. I get lots of breaks, and they do more cerebral work with me than they do with you. It's almost like they're trying to break you."

I thought about what he was saying. I didn't feel like it was true, but I didn't really know what they were doing with the others. I only knew what they did with me. I assumed they were easier on Maggie because she was younger.

"You're smart, Annie, so they don't need to work on your brain. You and Maggie, your training is all physical. They're monitoring how your organs react to the physical activities they run on you. You're different. Different than even me. You and Maggie. They see something better."

"That's crazy. We're just like everyone else from The Community."

"Maybe I'm wrong, but that's what people are saying."

"What people?"

"The Coats. I hear them talking. They don't think I'm listening, but I am, especially when I hear them talking about you and Maggie."

"They talk about us?"

It was insane to me that they spent more time with me and Maggie because there was something special about us.

Tiny knocked on the door then, and it was time for Kai to go. It was late, and I was tired anyway.

As he was leaving, he leaned down and kissed my cheek. Before I could react, he disappeared out my door. I held my hand to my face for a moment. It was warm where he had kissed it, his chin stubble scraping me slightly. I got a shiver, I'm not sure what from.

I thought about what he said. What could they be

looking for in us? What did we have that he didn't? He was a First Gen like we were. Born out in The Elements.

My thoughts went back to mine and Maggie's time out there. It was an easier time to me. I knew what was expected of me. Taking care of Maggie, making sure we didn't starve. Teaching her what I learned from Uncle Joe about the world, and what had happened. I didn't think too far into the future, because we never knew if we had one. It was day to day survival, and it was all we knew.

Now, my mind was filled with so many different things. So many different emotions. Talking to people in general was new for us, much less building a relationship with anyone other than each other. I found myself needing to talk to Hutch, and to Kai. Looking forward to interacting with the Coats, and the predictability of our days,. I was changing as fast as I saw Maggie change, and I didn't like it.

Chapter Fifteen

The next morning, Maggie and I got ready to start our day, and called for our escort. To my disappointment, Tiny showed up to take us to breakfast. When we got there, I scanned the cafeteria for Hutch. He wasn't anywhere to be found.

Kai was waving to us from a table at the far end. We made our way to him.

"Where's your shadow?"

"Huh?"

"Your handler. He didn't escort you today?"

"No, Tiny brought us."

"Trouble in paradise?"

"What?"

"Nothing, let's eat."

We ate quickly, drank our shakes, then separated to join our handlers in our respective ops.

Hutch wasn't in Op 8 when I got there. Dr. Kelly was there in his place.

"Hello, Anne."

"Hi Dr. Kelly. How are you?"

I was afraid to ask her where Hutch was.

"In case you're wondering where Hutch is, he's helping his father with something this week, and we're going to be doing something a little different with you today."

"What do you mean?"

"We want to do some brain activity testing with you."

"And how will you do that?"

"Sit, and we can get started."

She placed sensors on my temples, arms and chest near my heart. Then placed a strange visor over my eyes. It was only dark for a moment, before a remarkable scene came to life in front of me.

I was in a field. The greenest, lushest field. Colors so bright and clear, I didn't believe they existed anywhere at any time in the world.

"What are these images of?"

"This is what these lands looked like before The Shift."

My eyes were dancing, taking in all of what I saw. I

felt a breeze. I was certain it was my imagination. The grass moved, as if the wind that hit me moved it. I felt the warmth of the sun on my whole body. It had to be some kind of strange trick. I hadn't left Op 8.

"Tell me what you see, Anne."

"I am standing in the middle of a field. It's beautiful. I feel the sun beaming down on me, and a warm breeze on my face. How is this possible?"

"Tell me more. Do you hear anything?"

"I do. It's strange. A chirping maybe. But not like a bird. Well, not that I really even know what a bird sounds like."

"Stay with it, Anne. Do you smell anything?"

"I smell earth."

I was completely enthralled by the experience. I was hearing, seeing and smelling things for the first time in my life. I couldn't understand how she was doing it.

"Can you touch anything?"

I reached my hand out. I could see them extend out in front of me. I looked down, and I could see my body. I was in a yellow dress. I could see my feet. I was barefoot. I curled my toes, and I could feel the ground below me. I crouched to touch the tall grass I was standing in. I could feel the cool blades between my fingers. I could smell the freshness of nature around me. I looked up to see Hutch. He was suddenly right in front of me. He smiled. I reached out to take his hand. He took mine into his, and squeezed it tight. I felt safe. Safer than I had ever in my life felt. I looked up at the sun, squinting against its brightness. It seemed to get brighter, and I had to close my eyes.

When I opened them again, I was met with darkness. I wasn't in a field with Hutch. I wasn't in Op 8 with Dr. Kelly. I was in my room, in my bed.

It was as if the walls of our domicile were closing in on me. The wallpaper Hutch had picked out for us, the draperies over the simulated windows, the carpets that covered our floors. They all felt like they were trying to suffocate me. I was falling into a hole. A deep abyss of sadness. Nothing made sense anymore. I didn't know what I was doing, feeling, thinking. It was terrifying.

Was it all a dream? Did I not meet Dr. Kelly in Op 8?
Had those images I saw been real, once?

It felt so real. I could still smell the earth, feel the warmth, hear the birds chirping.

I closed my eyes and steadied my breathing. I tried to focus on my center, and pull myself from the grips of the dream.

I opened my eyes again, to an awful smell at my nose.

I was back in Op 8 with Dr. Kelly.

"What happened?"

"You fainted."

"Fainted? Why?"

How could I have seen, heard and smelled things I had never experienced before? What were they really doing to us? A sickening feeling of suspicion gripped me hard. I was suddenly overwhelmed with the need to escape. To pack Maggie up, and run back out into The Elements. I knew I needed to plan. I needed to be able to find my way around, before trying to blindly find our way out. And I knew convincing Maggie was not going to be easy. She had made friends, and fallen into a comfortable routine. She needed to come to the realization that things weren't right on her own.

My mind then went to Hutch. Would he understand what I was feeling? Would I tell him I wanted to leave? I was so confused, and I didn't like any of it.

"I want to show you something, Anne."

Dr. Kelly held two large pictures of what looked like images from inside a human body. They were black and white and transparent.

"This is a scan of one of our female technicians."

She held the picture up to the light, so I could see more definition. I could see the technicians heart and lungs.

"Now this is a scan of you, taken when you first came to The Combine."

"You mean when I was kidnapped, and dragged to The Combine?"

She ignored me, and held the picture up to the light.

I could see my heart, and my lungs.

"Yeah, so?"

She held the two pictures up, side by side.

There was a significant size difference between the two. My heart and lungs were much larger.

I didn't know what it meant.

Seeing my confusion Dr. Kelly continued.

"You and Maggie are special. Not all the First Gens show the evolution you two do. Your heart and lungs aren't the only things that are different. The exercise we just did, with the virtual reality glasses, was to see how much of your brain you access when your senses are stimulated. Your readings were well above anyone else here, which explains your almost perfect recall, after only a short period of observation.

"Your veins and arteries are wider than ours. Your nasal and ear canals, too. Your heart, lungs, your kidneys, liver and spleen, all larger. You don't have a gall bladder. Your small and large intestines are smaller, your bones are less dense. Your skin is thicker, your pupils are larger. The differences are extraordinary."

"So all these physical trials and testing, it was to see how Maggie and I have evolved?"

"We knew First Gens would have evolved in some way. We have First Gen Colonists who have evolved as well. But you and Maggie, your evolution seems to be accelerated."

"Why? Why us?"

"I don't have an explanation for that."

Chapter Sixteen

"Malakai, are you going to just stay here and let them dissect you?"

"What choice do I have?"

"We could break out. Leave here, me, you and Maggie."

"Oh yeah, and Hutch too?"

"What?"

"I see how cozy you two are."

"What are you talking about? He's a Coat."

"A Coat that you eat breakfast with every morning. Who you hang out with all day."

"I wouldn't exactly call what we do all day hanging out. He's part of all this. He's one of them."

I was shocked he was jealous. I was equally shocked I liked it. But what right did he have? I wasn't his girlfriend.

I decided to ignore what he was implying, and get back to my plan. If I could get Kai to agree to help me, maybe he could get Tiny to help too. I needed information. I needed to get a better layout of the compound, so I could design our exit plan.

"I'm talking about getting out of here. Escaping."

I lowered my voice, in case any Coats were within earshot.

"I know what you're talking about, and it's crazy. Why do you want to go back out there?"

"With everything you've heard, and what they're doing to us in here, you know this isn't for our benefit. Why should we stay?"

"Uh, I don't know, it's warm, there's endless amounts of food, we're not digging out of the garbage. I have never felt stronger or healthier in my life. Annie, it doesn't make sense to leave."

"We're lab rats, Kai."

"We're safe, Annie."

"I don't feel very safe."

"I think you're paranoid."

"Kai---"

Just as I was going to protest further, a Coat walked by, and we silenced so obviously I was surprised he didn't stop to ask what we were talking about.

I leaned closer to Kai, "When they find what they're looking for, what do you think they're going to do with us?"

"And how do you plan on getting out of this labyrinth?"

"Well, I was hoping we could enlist Tiny's help."

"I don't know Annie, he's broken some small rules for me, but this is major."

"I just need some blueprints, or layout of some sort of this place."

"Why don't you ask your boyfriend? I'm sure he has access to stuff like that."

"Really? What the hell is your problem?" I said it a lot louder than I had intended, and all heads turned in our direction.

"I have to go," I said, getting up from the table in a much more reasonable volume. "I'll talk to you later?"

"Yeah, whatever. Be careful Annie. Don't do anything stupid, I'll think about talking to Tiny."

"Only do it if you think it will help. If not, I'll figure it out on my own."

"Good luck convincing Maggie."

I wanted to turn back and yell at him for being so negative, but decided it wasn't worth it. I had hoped he would want to leave, like I did. I couldn't blame him for wanting to stay warm, and where the food is. But he had no right talking that way about Hutch.

Hutch.

What would I say to him?

The afternoon dragged. Hutch wasn't there. Some woman named Delia was my shadow. She had a lot of questions, and I didn't feel like talking so it frustrated her.

I wanted to talk to Maggie, and start planting seeds of doubt in her mind, so she would be on board when the time came.

I wanted to see Hutch.

I went back to our room after Delia finished the summary of our afternoon. Maggie wasn't there. She left me a note with a drawing of a white rose, saying sorry she wasn't there, she was at Abby's domicile, she would see me at dinner.

I didn't want to go to dinner. I called for an escort, hoping Hutch would show up. It was Tiny instead.

I tried talking to him as we walked, but he wasn't very receptive. I thought better of it and stopped trying.

"Tiny, do you think I could get a plate, and go back to my room? I don't feel like being here tonight."

Much to my great surprise, he agreed. I ordered my food, we waited for it, and he escorted me back to my room. I asked him to get word to Maggie and Kai where I was, so they wouldn't worry. He looked at me like I couldn't possibly have just asked him to do that for me. I was fairly certain they wouldn't get the message.

I sat in the living room, and ate at our coffee table. It was much nicer to be alone, than having to come up with things to talk about. I wondered why I hadn't thought to do it before. After lunch earlier, it was a welcome alternative. I didn't want to talk to Kai about my plans again yet, and I knew he would ask. He was probably going to stop by that night anyway, and I would have the chance to talk to him about it then.

I finished eating, and went to bed. It was early, but I didn't feel like doing anything else. I wanted to be in bed before Maggie could hit me with a thousand questions about where I was.

Sleep came easily.

Chapter Seventeen

It was 3:34 AM and Malakai had just left our room. I was still reeling from what happened while he was there. I replayed it in my head.

* * * * *

"Annie, I think we should talk."

"About what?"

"Us."

"Huh?"

"I like you Annie, I like you a lot. You're smart, funny, pretty and a hell of a fighter."

I didn't know what to say; my face flushed with embarrassment.

"I don't know what you have going on with Hutch ---"

"I told you, we're just friends," I interrupted, tired of where this conversation was going.

"Let me finish. I don't know what's going on with him, he clearly has feelings for you, but I think we belong together. You and me."

"Kai, I ---"

But he didn't let me finish, he kissed me. I didn't know what to do. I had never kissed a boy. It was strange, and exciting. I had really wanted him to kiss me, but was terrified of it at the same time. His arms were around me. He lifted my arms, to go around his neck. His stubble scratched my lips. I didn't know what I was doing. He seemed to. I didn't know what to do with my hands, so I left them where he placed them. I kissed him back, mimicking what he was doing to me. My head was spinning, Was this really happening? We kissed for what seemed like forever, when I finally decided I needed to come up for air. I pushed him away. More forcefully than I had intended.

"What's   wrong?"

"Nothing, I just needed to catch my breath."

"Oh, sorry."

"Nothing to be sorry for."

He leaned in for another kiss, and I stopped him. He looked at me, confused. I wasn't even sure why I stopped him.

"Kai, I don't know what just happened. I like you too. A lot. Probably more than I should, but this is crazy. I mean, what will happen next? What does all this mean?"

He looked hopeful. My heart was pounding and I wanted to cry.

"It means we like each other."

"And?"

"And, that's great!"

He all of a sudden looked young to me.

"We are prisoners here. We can't have a normal life together."

"We wouldn't have had that at home anyway, right? We're not normal, Annie. We are far from normal. I am so glad I met you. I wish I had met you out there, but I think everything happens for a reason, and we were brought here to find each other. I don't know what happens next. I haven't really thought about all that. I really just wanted you to know how I feel, and I really wanted to kiss you."

He held my hands, and looked intensely at me. It made me really uncomfortable. Maggie was in the next room. I knew I could fight if he tried anything more than I was comfortable with, and she would be out in a hot minute to help me. I shook my head, feeling bad for thinking he would ever do anything to hurt me.

"Annie, I'm gonna go. Please think about it. I think we could be really happy."

And then he left.

I laid on my bed. My mind was numb. My lips tingled, feeling raw from his rough stubble. I put my hand to my lips and held it there for a moment. I could smell him on my hands. My whole body felt different.

I didn't want to think about what it all meant. I wanted to sleep it away. I wasn't ready to deal with it.

Chapter Eighteen

"Hey Hutch, what's wrong? Where have you been? I've wanted so badly to talk to you. What happened?"

"Nothing."

"C'mon, what's up?"

"Anne, they're taking me off your case."

"What? Why?" The thought of not seeing him every day put a knot in my stomach I didn't understand.

"Father thinks I'm getting too, involved."

"Involved in what?"

"In you."

"What? That's crazy."

"Is it?"

"Well, yeah, isn't it?"

We were in Op 8, getting ready to start the day's trials. Hutch took my hand, and pulled me to the corner of the room.

"What are you doing?"

"The cameras can't see us here."

"What's wrong?" I asked, my concern growing.

"Anne, let's get away from here," he whispered.

"What? Where would we go?"

"Anywhere, I just want to be with you. But not here, not in this place. You wanna be with me, don't you?"

"I, uh...Hutch, wait. We can't just go. What about your father?"

"Screw my father. I don't care. Let's just go."

We stood silent, staring at each other. I searched his eyes. His brow was furrowed, and his big blue eyes begged me to say yes.

"Hutch?"

A voice came from the speaker above. I quickly moved in front of the camera.

"Dr. Kelly, I'm not feeling well. Is there any way I can take a day off?"

Hutch looked scared. There was a brief silence then Dr. Kelly's voice answered.

"Of course, Anne. You've been working really hard, and with little resistance. Hutch, please escort Anne to her room."

We walked back to my room in silence. I knew Maggie would be doing her trials. Our room would be empty. I motioned for Hutch to come in. He hesitated then came in.

I whispered for him to take my temperature, as I had feigned being sick.

"Can you turn the lights off? I feel a migraine coming on."

He looked at me, confused, then turned down the lights.

"Do you want something for the pain?"

"No, I think I just need to lie down."

He followed me into my bedroom. I shut the door behind him.

I knew they were watching my apartment, but there were no cameras in my bedroom. They assured me of that, and I had spent weeks sweeping mine and Maggie's bedrooms for anything that might resemble a camera or microphone.

"What are you doing Anne?"

"I have no idea. I just know I wanted to be alone with you."

He looked confused. My heart was leaping out of my chest. I had no clue how right Malakai was about Hutch and me.

"Did you mean what you said? That you want to run away from here?"

"Yes, I don't care where we go. Even if I have to live out in The Elements with you and Maggie. I want to be with you, Anne."

Was this really happening? My mind raced, my heart pounded. He was looking at me intensely. Not the way Kai looked at me the night before. This was better. I saw love in his eyes. I wasn't afraid. What was happening to my world? First Kai, now Hutch. I never even thought about boys before, and now two? We stood there for a long moment, without saying anything.

"When they gave me that picture of you, I memorized every line of your face. I didn't think I would ever meet you in person, and then you were here, and in my world, and you were so much more than what I imagined. Then they assigned me as your handler. I tried to fight it, I tried to ignore it, but I can't anymore. I love you, Anne." His stare penetrated my very soul. He looked almost in pain. His hands trembled as they reached for mine.

"I don't know what to say." I felt bad saying that, but I didn't know. I didn't know how to love. I didn't think I knew what it meant. His eyes searched mine. He was about to say something, but I silenced him with a kiss. I kissed him harder than I kissed Malakai. I didn't want to stop kissing him. I didn't know what was wrong with me.

A relieved smile spread across his handsome face. His smile lit up my entire world. Then his brow furrowed again.

"Wait, what about Malakai?" he asked, fear in his voice.

"What about him?"

"He can kill me."

I started to laugh. He looked at me, astonished at my

reaction.

"This is funny to you?"

It only made me laugh louder. I stopped myself, afraid they would hear me through the door of my bedroom. He was right. Malakai could kill him and probably would.

"I'm sorry. It's not funny," I apologized, unsuccessfully stifling my laughter. He looked so confused. I felt bad. "Hutch, you're probably right. Malakai would be really upset, and since he's from The Community and you're well, a Statie and a Coat, your chances in a fight aren't good. No offense."

"None taken."

I giggled.

He smiled. I was happy to see that. I was worried things would be weird, but they weren't at all. I felt completely comfortable and safe with him.

"I should go."

I didn't want him to leave, but knew he should. They would be looking for him.

"Okay. Will I see you later?" I looked up at him. I felt

something new. I felt truly happy.

"I promise, you will." He smiled, his arms around me. He kissed me goodbye, and left.

I spent the rest of the day lying in my bed, going over the events of the past twelve hours. I wanted to write in my journal, but I was afraid someone would find it, read it, and Hutch would get in trouble. I wondered where he'd gone after leaving me. I couldn't go back to trials after playing sick, and certainly didn't want to, so I sat in my room in the dark. Going back and forth between crying, smiling, laughing, wanting Hutch to come back, and feeling like I was going to throw up. In less than twenty-four hours, my life had completely changed, profoundly.

Maggie came home and checked on me, having been told I had skipped the day of trials. I told her I was fine, and she left me alone. She went to dinner and brought me back a plate food. Some kind of chicken, with rice and broccoli. I pushed the food around with my fork, but didn't eat any of it.

"Kai was looking for you at dinner. He's worried

about you."

I didn't respond. So many things were going through my head. I yearned for my old life, where I was in control, and I all I had to worry about was me and Maggie. I didn't have to deal with people, boys, or emotions. What was happening?

"Annie, what's going on?"

"What did you tell him?"

"Nothing, I don't know anything."

"I'm fine, I was just tired, they've been working us really hard and I needed a break."

"Have you seen Hutch?"

I hoped she wouldn't see my face flush, recalling my last encounter with him.

"Not since this morning."

"Is he okay?"

"Yeah, why?"

"He hasn't been your handler lately. I thought maybe something was wrong."

"They are reassigning him."

"What? Why?"

I shrugged.

"I think I know why."

I waited for her to continue.

"I think he's in love with you."

"What? Don't be ridiculous." My heart was in my throat. How could something be so apparent to everyone else but me.

"C'mon, Annie, you don't see the way he looks at you? If that isn't love, I don't know what is. I hope I can have someone look at me like that someday."

My little sister was growing up too fast.

"You will, baby."

I opened my arms to give her a hug. She ran to me. We hugged for a long time. Swaying back and forth, and laughing as we almost fell off my bed. She looked gigantic to me. Everything about her was growing up. The way she looked was only the start of it. The way she carried herself, the way she spoke, even the look in her eyes. I longed for a simpler time, back at our campsite playing chess, making each other laugh, exploring the ruins around us. When she was my baby sister, depending on me. Her independence terrified me. We barely saw each other anymore. I missed her. I didn't want to let her go, but she squirmed away from me giggling and ran to her room. Despite having skipped trials, I was exhausted. Alone again, I closed my eyes, picturing Kai then Hutch. It was clear in my mind and in my heart. I didn't love Kai. I drifted off to sleep, knowing what I needed to do.

* * * * *

Malakai knocked at his usual time, and my stomach jumped. I knew I was going to have to tell him about Hutch. I promised myself I would tell him right away, so there was no confusion. I had made my decision.
He walked in and I blurted it out quickly, like I was ripping a bandage off.
"What?" He looked as if I had punched me in the gut.
"I don't know what happened, when it happened. It was not something I wanted to happen, believe me."

"You're *with* him now?" He said it with such disgust, I flinched. "You said you were just friends."

"I didn't know what I felt about him. You seemed to know before I even did."

The look in Malakai's face frightened me. There was a darkness in his eyes I had never seen before. The rage was unmistakable. I suddenly feared what he might do. "How could you do this?"

He wasn't being reasonable. He grabbed my wrist, and twisted it so severely, I cried out in pain.

I was terrified. Maggie was in the next room. I started to call for her, but Malakai put his hand over my mouth. His hand tightened over my face. I squealed in pain. I heard Maggie call for me, asking if I was alright. I wanted desperately to answer her, but Malakai had a vice like grip on me. I screamed, the sound muffled by his large hand. He forced me into my bedroom, locking the door behind him. He threw me on the floor hard, taking my breath away. Before I could recover, he was on top of me. His strength was unfathomable. I had fought many men, but his strength, his rage, made him seem superhuman.

Maggie was banging on the door, screaming for me. I wanted to tell her to run. Run and get help. Malakai's strength overpowered me. He hit me with such force, I felt my nose break. He was on top of me, putting all of his weight on me, I heard the crack of my ribs breaking. I couldn't fight. I was frozen with fear, not knowing what he was going to do to me.

He hit me over and over. I stopped struggling. There was nothing I could do.

Maggie finally got the door open. I looked up at her, wanting to tell her to run. No words came. I couldn't imagine the sight she saw coming in. I watched her face turn from concern to fury. She flew at Malakai. He quickly turned his rage on her. He was pummeling her. I couldn't do anything to help her. I watched him unleash his fury on her, and laid there helpless to do anything. I was barely breathing. He had beaten me so severely, I could barely move. Out of the corner of my blood-filled eye, I saw the call button hanging from my bedside. I summoned all the strength and will I had left to save my sister, and somehow managed to reach it. I pressed it repeatedly, with a broken hand, pain radiating through my entire existence. I wanted to scream. Only a gurgled cough escaped.

Maggie stopped reacting to Malakai's strikes. I couldn't tell if she gave up, or passed out, or worse.

The first to respond was Hutch. I didn't see what happened. I was fading in and out of consciousness. I saw only flashes of Maggie and Hutch and Malakai. There was shouting, and the sound of metal hitting flesh and bone, then silence.

I looked up to see Hutch holding Uncle Joe's baseball bat. My vision blurred. My body was plump and swollen from endless injuries. His face twisted in horror at the sight of me. He was covered in blood. I wanted to answer him, but no words came. I saw Maggie lying next to Malakai. She was moving. Malakai was not.

"What did you do, Hutch?"

He dropped the bat, running to my side. My face felt swollen, I could hear it in my speech. Blood dripped from my nose into my mouth, and sent me into a coughing fit.

"Don't worry, you're going to be alright." He was on the floor with me, cradling me in his arms.

"Maggie?" I reached out for her.

"They're coming, Anne, they're on their way. Everything is going to be fine."

He sounded far away.

Darkness crept into the corners of my eyes. I felt someone lift me up onto a stretcher. I was taken to the infirmary. I could see Maggie lying in a bed nearby. She had wires attached to everywhere.

I felt myself drift in and out of consciousness. At one point, the sight of a broken Maggie was too much for me to bear. I didn't know if it was real or a dream.

I started screaming, screaming uncontrollably. Pain ripped through every part of my being. A Coat appeared, trying to give me a shot of something. I sat up in my bed, and took him by the throat. His hands grabbed my wrist in an attempt to loosen my grip.

"Anne, no. Let him go."

It was Dr. Kelly. I didn't want to listen, I believed he was trying to hurt me.

"Anne, he's trying to give you a sedative. You're badly injured. We need to tend to your wounds."

I released my grip, and the Coat fell to the floor.

"What's happening?"

"Anne, please calm down. Lay back. you've been attacked. We're still trying to piece together the events of the evening. Please try not to talk or move. You're injuries are severe and numerous. Maggie is also badly injured. Malakai is dead."

Her words hung in the air, and echoed through my soul. I felt the sting of a needle in my arm, and everything went black.

Chapter Nineteen

"Anne, can you hear me? Anne?"

Dr. Kelly. She sounded far away. My eyelids felt like lead, so heavy. I couldn't open my mouth. My arms and legs were immobilized. Pain coursed through me.

"Anne, you've been asleep for a few days now."

I tried to sit up quickly, shocked by what she said, but that was a mistake. The pain was unbearable, the room spun, and things immediately went dark again.

* * * * *

I opened my eyes to a blank white ceiling. I wasn't in my domicile. I couldn't remember where I was. I tried to sit up.

"Anne, please don't try to get up."

It was Dr. Kelly. I heeded the warning.

Unable to speak, I stared up at her with so many questions.

"We have been keeping you heavily sedated. Your injuries were vast and critical. You have a broken jaw. We have wired your mouth shut. You have six broken ribs, a fractured clavicle, a broken nose and cheek bone, your left arm and right leg are broken."

I remembered what happened, and flinched. I tried to assess any pain, but felt nothing.

"Do you remember what happened?"

I nodded.

"It's been three weeks since the incident."

Three weeks? Where was Maggie? Hutch? The last thing I remember was Dr. Kelly telling me Malakai was dead. Did I kill him? Did Maggie? Then I remembered the image of Hutch holding the baseball bat.

I tried to sit up. Dr. Kelly put a hand on my shoulder. She looked very serious. I was certain I didn't want to hear what she had to say.

"Anne, please don't try to get up. I know you must have a lot of questions. Maggie is in the next room. She sustained similar injuries to you. There was bleeding in her brain we couldn't control. She's in a medically induced coma. Do you understand what that means?"

I knew what a coma was, but wasn't capable of dealing with the information. Tears sprang to my eyes. I nodded.

Through my wired jaw, I managed to say, "Hutch."

"Hutch has been arrested."

I looked at her confused.

"He killed Malakai, Anne. They take murder very seriously here. Even if it was self defense, or in an attempt to protect you and Maggie. He was arrested and processed."

Malakai was dead. Hutch had killed him. Killed him for hurting me, for hurting Maggie. He killed him with Uncle Joe's baseball bat. What did she mean by processed? My mind replayed the nightmare in perfect recall. I felt the weight of an elephant on my chest, and suddenly couldn't breathe. My bandaged hand went to my neck, to signal to Dr. Kelly I couldn't breathe.

"Anne? Anne, can you breathe?"

I shook my head frantically. My whole body convulsed. I didn't have any control. I was racked with pain.

"She's seizing! Push 4 CC's of Ativan, and call Dr. Sanford." They gave me a shot of something, and everything went black again.

* * * * *

There was music playing, somewhere far away. I couldn't make out what it was, something classical. I sat at a grand table, with a large bountiful feast before me. There were many people at the table. I couldn't make out any faces. They looked to be smiling, but were simply a blur. At the end of the table, I could see Hutch. He looked handsome and strong. He was whispering something to Maggie. She was standing next to him, looking more beautiful than I had ever seen her. She wore a gorgeous, ornate dress made from gold and shimmering jewels. She looked like a princess.

I tried to speak, but was silenced by a hand over my mouth and nose. My attacker came from behind. The people at the table didn't seem to notice. I was pulled back, and dragged out of the room. I didn't have the energy to fight back. I simply let myself be taken.

It felt like hours before the dragging stopped, even though I knew it couldn't have been. I was dropped onto a cold metal floor, in the middle of a small empty room. A naked light bulb hung from the center of a white ceiling. A rusted chain swung from it. It was the only source of light. It was bright. I had to squint. I shielded my eyes with my hand. I tried to speak again, but no sound came. I tried to look around to see my kidnapper. There was no one there.

"Help!" I finally managed to croak out. My voice bounced off the metal walls, sounding hollow.

No one answered.

I pulled my knees to my chest, feeling suddenly cold. The ornate dress I was wearing was ripped and tattered. I could hear what sounded like a siren, or alarm. It was muffled, far off in the distance. It started to get louder. And louder. Soon, it was as if it was in the room with me. I had to cover my ears. It was deafening. I closed my eyes, willing it to stop.

Everything was fuzzy and confusing.

An image of Hutch appeared to me. I couldn't be sure if it was a dream, or if he was really there.

"Everything is going to be okay, I promise."

The image of him started to float away. I reached out for him, but he disappeared into the darkness.

I felt very tired. I closed my eyes. A feeling of floating, and then falling overcame me. I reached my arms out, grasping only air. A sudden panic filled me. I opened my eyes, I was back in my hospital bed at The Combine. Dr. Kelly was sitting next to me. She looked to be sleeping. She seemed to be genuinely concerned about me, which I found strange.

I felt the familiar set up of an IV attached to my arm. My mouth was dry, no longer wired shut. I opened my mouth, moving my jaw in a circular motion. My stomach grumbled loudly.

I remembered what Dr. Kelly told me the last time I was awake. Maggie was still in a coma.

"Dr. Kelly?"

Dr. Kelly was quickly at my side.

"Anne? Oh thank goodness. How are you feeling?"

"Hungry, and thirsty."

She handed me a glass of water, and raised my bed slowly, so I could sit up.

"Maggie?"

"She's still not awake. Anne, you need to take it easy. With your injuries, we made the decision to induce a coma for you as well, so you could heal."

"How long is a while?"

"We were not optimistic you would come out of it."

"How long?"

"Twelve weeks."

Twelve weeks? I lost three months. Closing my eyes, I tried to remember anything I could. I remembered Malakai attacking me. He was dead, Hutch had killed him, and Maggie was in a coma. My hunger pangs churned into nausea from the memory.

"What happened to Hutch?"

Dr. Kelly hesitated. I could tell she was afraid of my reaction.

"He was processed."

"What does that even mean?"

"Murder holds a very severe punishment, Anne. He was expelled."

"Expelled? Like cast out?"

"Yes, that's correct."

"What?! He'll never survive."

The thought of him out in The Elements terrified me.

"We have people looking out for him."

She paused, and looked very serious.

"Anne, there's something else I have to tell you."

I couldn't imagine what else there could be.

"Anne, you're pregnant."

Chapter Twenty

"What? How?!?"

I looked down and could see a slight bulge in my belly I didn't have before.

"Anne, you were in a coma. There was very little chance you would survive."

"So? What does that have to do with anything?" I could feel my breathing quicken. I was starting to hyperventilate. My head was spinning. I couldn't comprehend what was happening.

Dr. Kelly took a deep breath.

"Anne, I told you, our Estates are failing. We need to find a way to survive out in The Elements. You, Malakai, and Maggie, you're First Gens born out in a world we have never had to survive in. Hutch is a First Gen, born in The Combine. You have all evolved to adapt. Imagine what we could learn from a Second Gen. Either one born of two Commons, or one born of a Common and a Colonist? We didn't know if you would ever wake up. We had to try. One specimen was successful. We don't know which combination yet. It is too early to accurately determine who the father is. We were waiting for the first trimester to complete. When we know, we can learn so much."

As what she was saying sunk in, I understood. They thought I was going to die, so they were using me as a vessel to grow a super human.

"How could you?" I screamed.

I leapt out of the bed. I ripped all the wires from my body. I wrapped my hands around Dr. Kelly's neck.

Two Coats were immediately surrounding me, pulling me from her.

"I could be carrying Malakai's baby? I'll kill you!"

With one hand still around Dr. Kelly's throat, I sent one Coat sailing across the room. I was about to take out the second Coat, when Tiny walked in.

"Anne, stop!"

His voice boomed through the room. It was the first time I had ever heard him speak.

I stopped fighting, and dropped Dr. Kelly. She retreated to the corner of the room, coughing, holding her throat. Her perfect hair was tousled, a terrified look on her face.

"What right do you have? Was this your plan all along?"

"Anne, you have to understand ---"

"Understand? Are you serious right now? I have to understand. You've violated me beyond anything I could possibly understand!"

I was crying, which annoyed me. Tiny ushered me back to the bed. I let him. I was suddenly very tired.

"You had no right. Get out. All of you, get out."

Tiny lead them all out.

Staring down at my stomach, I ran my hand across it. It looked strange. The more I thought about what they had done, the more enraged I became. How could they do that to me?

I looked to my stomach again in sheer disgust. Fueled by raw hatred, I started punching it, pulling and clawing at it. Willing it to die. I was crying uncontrollably. Tears were streaming down my face. I screamed, picking up anything I could throwing it to the floor, or against a wall. There was so much rage in me. I thrashed around, a hurricane destroying everything in my wake. I found a scalpel in one of the drawers. I raised it high above my head.

As I did, I caught a glimpse of myself in one of the machines that had survived my fury. What if this child was Hutch's?

Chapter Twenty-One

I dropped the scalpel, then crumpled to the floor. My emotions were overflowing. I could barely breathe between sobs. I needed Maggie. I needed to see Hutch. A memory of my mom being sick a lot when she was pregnant with Maggie came to mind. Would that happen to me? I had no idea what to expect. I was certain they didn't have my best interest in mind. They needed a solution to their problem, and I held the key. I wanted Hutch back. How would he ever survive out there? The thought of it horrified and infuriated me. I pulled myself back up.

"Hey! I know you can see me. I want to see Dr. Kelly or someone else in charge, right now!"

I yelled, my focus on the camera in the corner of the ceiling.

The door slid open to reveal Tiny, standing next to a man I recognized, but hadn't seen since the first day I woke up in The Combine.

Turning away from them, I took a deep breath to calm

myself, then turned to face them.

"Dr. Sanford."

"Hello, Anne. You remember me."

"Yes, well, they've done a lot of work on my memorization skills in here since I arrived."

"I understand what you must be feeling, and the questions you most undoubtedly have."

"I want you to find Hutch and bring him back here."

"I'm afraid that's not possible."

"Well, you better make it possible, or the little solution to your big problem you've cooked up inside of me is going bye bye."

I showed them the scalpel, then placed it to my wrist.

"Anne, please don't do anything rash."

Dr. Sanford was a short man, with a receding hairline of black hair. He wore glasses only rimmed on top. He wore the standard white lab coat, with a tightly knotted tie, around a white collared shirt. I watched as a bead of sweat ran down his left temple.

"Do as I say, or I will kill myself and take all your hopes and dreams with me."

Tiny stepped forward.

"Back off, Tiny."

"I'm not going to let anything happen to you, Anne. Please give me the scalpel." It was strange hearing his voice.

"Get Hutch. Find him, and bring him back here. Now!"

I pierced the skin on my left wrist, letting the blood drip to the floor.

"Okay, okay." Dr. Sanford conceded throwing his hands up in the air, "Tiny, go. Do as she says."

"No one comes back in here until he's back." I ordered, threatening to cut myself further.

"Yes, yes, of course."

They both scurried out of the room. I found a bandage, and placed it over the fresh wound I had created. I didn't feel the pain. I didn't feel anything. I couldn't wrap my head around it all. I wanted to run. Run and find Maggie, run out into The Elements and find Hutch. I was suddenly tired again.

Laying back on the bed, I could feel sleep take me

again.

Chapter Twenty-Two

I opened my eyes, still feeling exhausted. I sat up, and surveyed the destroyed room around me. They did as I asked, and left me alone. I was surprised, considering how important I now was, and the fact I had just woken out of a three month coma. I was certain they still watched me for the entirety of my sleep.

I looked to the door in time to see it slide open. Expecting to see a Coat, or Dr. Kelly, my eyes filled with tears when I saw him. He looked terrible. He was thin and pale. He had clearly taken a beating from The Elements. He wore the same whites the rest of us Commons wore upon being brought into The Combine. He was one of us now.

"Anne, they told me you were dead."

We cried as we hugged, holding each other as close as we could, afraid to let go and lose each other again.

"I love you, Hutch."

"I love you too, Anne"

"I'm so glad you're here."

He cupped my face with his hands. Smiling through tears, he spoke, his voice less than a whisper, "I'm so happy you're alive."

We kissed softly. I felt safe, safer than I had ever felt, and never wanted to let go.

"Look at you, you're a mess." I said, smiling through my tears, running my hand through his still wet hair.

"You look beautiful. Exactly as I imagined you the whole time I was out there."

"How did you survive?"

"I had help. They dropped me at your campsite. I guess they thought if I was familiar with it, it would be easier. They were watching me. Anytime things got really rough, somehow a solution would reveal itself. I can't believe what you and Maggie endured for all those years. I am so sorry."

"How is Maggie?"

"She hasn't woken up."

I started to cry harder, imagining my life without my baby sister.

"Hutch, what have they told you?" I asked, wondering if they had told him about the baby. The reason he was allowed to return.

"What do you mean?"

"Hutch, I'm pregnant."

His eyes went wide. I could see him process the information.

"They did it. They actually did it."

"What are you talking about?"

"Those bastards!"

"You knew what they were planning?"

"They were injecting Malakai with testosterone in preparation. When I found out what they were planning, I refused to participate and threatened to tell you if they didn't stop. They swore they wouldn't do it."

"I'm so glad he's dead."

"Anne, listen to me, Malakai was not himself. They had him pumped with so much testosterone, that day in particular. He wasn't supposed to see you, or anyone that night."

"I can't believe you're defending him."

"I'm not. I hate what happened to you. I am trying to make you see, it wasn't his fault. That monster who attacked you, it wasn't who Malakai was. I really do think he loved you."

I couldn't forgive him, even with an excuse. He almost killed me and Maggie.

"I really hope it's yours. I wouldn't be able to handle it if it's his."

"What?"

"They said only one specimen was successful, and they don't know which of you is the father."

"Which one of us?"

"You, or Kai."

Hutch loosened his arms around me, a look of confusion on his face. He backed away from me, almost stumbling. He clearly didn't know he could be the father. Of course they didn't tell him that part. These people, playing God, deciding our fate, our lives, without our interest or input. I felt the rage bubbling up inside me again.

"Hutch?"

He looked at me. His eyes searching mine. I was desperate to know what he was thinking. Was he as angry as I was? Was he so changed from being banished, he couldn't process what was happening? He looked so frail. His eyes sunken, his collar bones protruding. His skin so horribly pale and thin. He hadn't done well out there. I watched as his mind tried to fully comprehend the information I was giving him. It was clear he had no idea they had planned this for him as well. His silence was unnerving. I thought he might run, and leave me again. The thought of it made my breath catch.

Before I could speak again, he pulled me close to him and wrapped his arms around me. I closed my eyes, relief washing over me.

Chapter Twenty-Three

"Anne," Dr. Kelly stood in the doorway, flanked by two Coats, undoubtedly there for her protection. A bandage was wrapped around her neck, where I had tried to squeeze the life out of her. I felt a spark of guilt that quickly extinguished, remembering why I attacked her.

"You both have been through a great deal physically, and we need to get you both some rest. Especially you, Hutch. We would like you to return to your domiciles. We have set up your spaces to support what we need to get you both back to health. We know you will be more comfortable in your own beds.

"Hutch, good to see you back."

"Dr. Kelly." Hutch nodded, acknowledging her without taking his eyes from mine.

"Are you kidding?" I exclaimed, astonished she would come back and attempt to give us orders.

"Anne, it's okay. She's right, we need to heal. I know I would like to sleep in a real bed again."

It was amazing to me how he could remain so calm after everything.

"Thank you for understanding, Hutch."

"Dr. Kelly, please don't mistake my cooperation with understanding. What you've done here, what you're doing to us, it's completely unacceptable and utterly unforgivable."

He sounded strong and confident. The outside *had* changed him. I could see experience in his eyes.

"We will have Tiny escort you back to your rooms."

"Can we stay together, at mine and Maggie's place? There are two bedrooms there," I asked, not wanting to be alone.

I watched as Dr. Kelly considered it. Hesitantly, she nodded to her two Coat escorts. They disappeared, understanding they needed to change the set up accordingly.

"Tiny will be here shortly. I will check on you later. I truly am happy you're back and safe, Hutch."

She touched her neck, then looked at me.

"I understand, Anne, why you did this."

Neither of us responded. She turned on her heel and disappeared out into the hall.

Hutch put his hands on my shoulders.

"Everything is going to be okay, I promise."

Chapter Twenty-Four

Down the metal corridors we walked in silence. The halls seemed different to me. They didn't have the same cold feeling about them. They had a familiarity that was comforting to me. I never thought I would feel that way about anything inside The Combine. Tiny didn't say a word the entire walk back to our domicile. I couldn't tell if he was angry or sorry about the events.

The door opened, and I felt like I had spent a lifetime away. Hutch and I stepped in. I remembered the last time he and I were together there. So much had changed since then.

To our surprise, Tiny followed us in. He stood with his back to the cameras.

"You two have to get out of here." He whispered.

"I'm happy to have you both back." He said louder, deliberately for those who may be listening.

Hutch and I looked at each other, then back at Tiny. He placed his hand on one of each of our shoulders.

"I will help you, but you have to leave here. I have seen what they have planned for you both, and the child you are carrying. It will take time. I need you both to be patient, and cooperate with everything." Whispering again, we had to strain to hear him.

"Now get some rest!" Loudly, and I thought, a bit too cheerful. An actor, Tiny was not.

We didn't say anything. I had so many questions.

"Nod if you understand."

We both nodded.

"Maggie?" I asked barely audible.

Tiny hung his head, his shoulders sagged, defeated. "I don't think she's ever going to wake up, Anne."

"Can I see her?"

"Tomorrow."

I didn't cry. I didn't know how to feel. It wasn't what I wanted to hear, but exactly what I expected.

"Do as I say, and I will take care of everything else."

One last whisper, then loudly, "Goodnight, you two."

With that, he left us confused, staring at each other.

Hutch looked very tired. Too tired to even speak. I

felt inexplicably fine, considering I had been in a coma, only being used as an incubator, less than twelve hours before. We didn't dare talk about what Tiny just said, though I knew we both wanted to.

"You're bleeding."

I looked down, and saw the bandage around my wrist soaked through with blood from the self inflicted wound. I hadn't noticed it. Hutch found the med kit and redressed it.

"I need to sleep, Anne."

"Of course. Go, I'm fine. I'm sure some Coats will be here soon, to hook us up to things."

As if on cue, two Coats showed up at our door. Taking Hutch to Maggie's room, and me to mine, they hooked us up to the equipment waiting for us there. I caught a last look at Hutch before they closed the door to Maggie's room, and smiled at him. He smiled back, exhaustion and pain in his eyes, as the door slid closed.

I followed the other Coat to my room. He hooked me up to the machines there. It was nice to be in my own bed again. I never thought I would ever think that way.

The whole process took about ten minutes, but felt like an eternity. I just wanted to be left alone. Left to think about what was happening to me. I had a human growing inside of me. This was not my choice. This was not the life I wanted.

Tiny was right. We needed to leave. They didn't deserve this child. Whether it was Malakai's or Hutch's it didn't matter. It wasn't theirs.

I laid on my bed, with wires attached to me. An IV in my arm. The only light coming from the machines, beeping and whirring around me.

Chapter Twenty-Five

"It was miserable. So very cold. I'm not sure if they were trying to be ironic when they left me at your campsite. There was a fire lit for me, and they did give me Element appropriate clothes. Tiny brought me out himself. It broke my heart to see first hand how you and Maggie lived. It was as nice a space as you could have made for yourselves. Most of your things had been looted through. I didn't get the impression any other Pride had tried living there. Anyway. they handed me a week's worth of rations and left."

Sitting in the dark in Maggie's room, each of us tethered to an IV pole, Hutch told his story. We had only tried to sleep for a couple of hours before I heard shouting, he was having a nightmare. I rolled my IV pole to his bedside to wake him. He woke up, and started talking about his experience out in The Elements.

"I guess it could have been worse." I said, shaking my

head. I wondered what a week's worth of rations to a Statie would be.

"So, I guess, now you know what our life was like."

"No, Anne, not at all. The first night I didn't sleep at all. I knew they were watching me. I hoped if they saw me in trouble, they would intervene. I always had that possibility in the back of my mind that if something happened, I would have help. So no, I have no idea what you guys went through. They left me there with what I needed to survive for a week. A week according to The Combine. I imagine it was a bounty compared to what you and Maggie had. "

"Yeah, I suppose." I nodded, and stared at him. I could see it in his eyes. His time out in The Elements had changed him.

"The sky was always gray, the ground had no give. I had to learn how to build a fire. I went a little further out everyday to memorize my way to The Estates. I learned how to scavenge, and dig through the garbage. The Commons were not kind. One Pride came in, beat me up, and took almost all my food. When it was all gone, I ate from the garbage. The first time. I got horribly sick. I screamed into the cameras and begged them to let me back in. I cried, and prayed for death."

I watched him remember. He stared past me now, his eyes brimming with tears. His chin quivered. I wanted to take his pain away. I took his hand in mine.

"When they told me you were dead." His voice trailed of. He took my hands in his, and cried harder than I had ever seen a boy cry.

"It's okay now, you don't have to tell me anymore. You're here with me now. You're safe."

Knowing there were no cameras in Maggie's room, we finally talked about what Tiny said.

"Is this what you want Anne? To go back out there?"

"I don't know. I do know we can't stay here. They're going to dissect me and it."

"Maybe it won't be so terrible," he said, looking away from me. He understandably did not want to go back.

"Tiny said it was going to take time. We have to find out what he has planned. He told us to play along and cooperate. That's what we'll do. We won't be going out there anytime soon."

That seemed to make him feel better.

We spent the rest of the night holding each other in Maggie's bed. He didn't have anymore nightmares. I didn't dream at all.

* * * * *

The next morning, Tiny was at our door, with breakfast, and a note. I hid it in the bathroom. After eating, and a visit from Dr. Kelly, I retrieved the note, and we went into Maggie's room to read it.

You both have tracking nodes implanted behind your left ears. We have to disable the trackers before you leave. Everyone involved in The Savior Project has one. We have to get you to The Bloch Estate. My cousin Daryl Tyson can do it.

Hutch and I both touched the back of ears. I could feel the slightest little bump. I never would have noticed it.

"What are we going to do?" I asked.

"We will figure it out. With Tiny's help, we'll figure it out.

Chapter Twenty-Six

Sitting on the couch in my domicile, Hutch and I held hands, waiting to find out what would happen to us next.

Dr. Kelly was recovering from my attack on her. Tiny had taken on the role of keeper for us, feeding us information on our escape whenever he could.

My wounds had completed healed. I could feel movement from the baby growing inside me. It terrified and appalled me.

The paternity test was performed that morning.

"Whatever happens Anne, whatever the result, I love you, and will take care of you, and the child."

I believed him.

Dr. Kelly had said she would bring the results to us in person.

"Anne, marry me."

"What?"

"Let's get married. Let's be a real family with this child."

"I, I don't know what to say."

"Say yes."

"Yes! Yes, of course. Are you sure?"

"I have never been more sure about anything in my life."

He got down on one knee in front of me.

"This was my mother's." He pulled a small ring from his pocket. It was gold, with a small sparkly diamond in the center.

"Anne, will you marry me?"

"Yes, yes, I will."

He slipped the tiny ring onto my finger, and it fit perfectly. I pulled him up from the floor, and we kissed softly. I admired my newly decorated hand while we embraced.

"Anne?" Dr. Kelly walked in.

We looked at her. I instinctively hid my hand from her. I was holding my breath.

"Congratulations, you two, you're going to be parents. It's a girl."

Hutch hugged me tight. Knowing it was a girl made it

more real to me. I couldn't call it an "it" anymore. I could name her and picture her now. It truly changed everything. Thank God she was Hutch's.

"Dr. Kelly, Anne and I would like to get married."

She looked at me. I smiled and nodded, showing her the ring Hutch had just given me.

She shook her head, taking a step back.

My heart sank. Then she smiled.

"I think that would be lovely."

"Can we go see Maggie now? "

"Of course you can."

She left, and we went into Maggie's room, which for all intents and purposes was just Hutch's room now.

"Was that believable?" Hutch asked, looking anxious.

"Totally! You were fantastic."

"And you looked completely surprised!"

We laughed at it all. It was funny.

I was certain anyone who might have been watching us would believe the proposal and my reaction. The only variable was whether or not Dr. Kelly would let us. We had her blessing. Now we had to plan a believable Statie wedding in the Bloch Estate.

Chapter Twenty-Seven

Maggie looked so peaceful. Her breathing was even, rhythmic. Monitors surrounded her, whirring and beeping. Hutch held my hand as we approached her.

Her injuries healed. Small scars on her face were already fading. She just looked like she was sleeping. I wanted to wake her and hug her and tell her everything would be alright.

How could everything have gone so horribly wrong so fast? Again, I found myself crying. I never cried so much in my entire life. Hutch said it could be from the hormones from the pregnancy. I hated not being in control of my emotions.

I took Maggie's hand into mine. It was warm.

"Mags, it's Annie."

I knew she wouldn't respond, but I was hoping she would hear me. Hutch pulled a chair up for me, to sit next to her bed. The room was dimly lit. I rested my head on her arm. I could feel her breathing.

"I love you, baby girl. I wish I could talk to you. I have so much to tell you."

"Tell her Anne. She can hear you." Hutch put his hands on my shoulders.

"Hutch is here. He asked me to marry him. You know how we used to have pretend weddings with you and Louie? He's here by the way, your bear. He's sitting on the other side of you, looking pathetic."

I laughed through my tears at the beat up old bear, sitting, head cocked to one side, as if it was looking up at Maggie.

I sat chatting with my sister for another hour. I didn't realize how much I missed her, and needed to talk to her. I wished she would wake up. I wanted to see her eyes, needed to hear her voice. I want to tell her everything we were planning, but didn't dare. We had to keep up the ruse for our plan to work.

I suddenly felt very tired. My eyes felt heavy. This pregnancy thing was awful.

I looked at Hutch. He had been so patient with me. "We can go."

I kissed Maggie's cheek, and told her I would back real soon.

Her little friend Abby was coming in for a visit as we were leaving.

"Hi Annie," she smiled, and waved to us.

"Hi Abby, how are you?" I had forgotten all about her. She must have been so lonely without Maggie.

"I miss her."

"Me too, honey. If you need anything, please let us know."

"I will, thanks. Bye."

I wondered where they were in the process with Abby. If she was found to be "special", like Maggie and I. If I could have figured out a way to get her out too, I would have. For now, we needed to execute our plan.

Chapter Twenty-Eight

Once they felt I was back to health, they put me back on a routine. Hutch was not my handler, for obvious reasons. They wanted him to move back to his own Domicile. We protested, and they let us have our way. I didn't want to be alone, and it gave us plenty of time to plan our escape. I met his father, Dr. Edgar Alexander. We had the most awkward exchange I've ever experienced. He was not pleased Hutch had proposed. He said we were too young. I laughed out loud when he said it. Of course we were too young. Did he think either of us wanted to be in the situation we were in? What he really wanted to say was he didn't want his son to marry a Common. I guess I couldn't really blame him. Despite the fact that me and the baby I was carrying was going to save his kind, he still thought of me as below them.

He was happy Hutch was back, and had become an important part of The Savior Project. I could tell

Hutch desperately wanted to please his father. All in all, it was good. For now. Soon we would be free, and his father would most definitely not be proud.

Chapter Twenty-Nine

Our wedding became the event of The Estates. The Coats, men and women, were thrilled, and would all be there. The heads of all The Estates would be invited. One of the designers from the Taxter Estate volunteered to design my dress. Others got involved, donating flowers and a wedding cake, the suit Hutch would wear. It was quickly spinning out of control. Tiny thought it was a good thing. A strong distraction for us to execute our plan. We would use it all to our advantage. They even wanted Hutch and I to make an appearance at all The Estates. Their future depended on us, and they wanted to celebrate us. I had witnessed a handful of weddings out in The Elements. They were very low key, quick, and performed by an Elder. There was never a party after it.

I was swept up into the whirlwind. They wanted everything to happen quickly, before I was too far along. They even made plans for me to visit the

Taxter Estate for a dress fitting. A dress fitting. The words were so outrageously foreign to me. The entire experience was insane. I didn't know how to feel about it all. Hutch seemed to enjoy it far more than I did. He welcomed the attention. It made him feel important. It gave him confidence, pride. I liked seeing him like that.

They monitored everything I did, all of the food I ate. All of my meals were pre-packaged, and I was drinking a shake with breakfast, lunch and dinner with two additional shakes throughout the day. Dr. Kelly said it was important for my health, and the health of my daughter. I went along with it all, knowing we had an end game.

The best part of all was that they took such good care of me, their savior. Most of what I asked for, I got, without argument. And not just from the people in The Savior Project. People from all The Estates. We were being sent things for the wedding, and for the baby. The head of The Wilkes Estate, Thomas Wilkes the Fourth himself, offered us their most exclusive Domicile to live in after we got married.

The more I thought about it, the crazier it all was. I decided to simply not think about it. I let things transpire around me. I was afraid they might suspect something, with how cooperative we were. To be safe, I threw in a few days of defiance here and there for good measure.

Tiny said everything was on track, and no one suspected anything. They were all too distracted by the wedding, and the planned events leading up to it. He was our eyes and ears behind the scenes. We weren't completely clear on all the things he had to take care of for us, but we would be forever grateful. We prayed they would never discover how he helped us.

"I got a gold rattle today."

"A what?"

"A gold rattle. It's for the baby to shake, to keep her

entertained."

"Seriously?"

"Yes, Maggie had one that was plastic, when she was a baby."

"I also got this." I held up what I assumed was some kid of pajama. It was satin and lace and wouldn't cover much of anything for anyone who wore it. I thought it was funny. "The note that came with it said, 'for the wedding night'."

The look on Hutch's face was equally funny. His eyes went wide, he blushed a deep crimson, and he quickly looked away.

"Anne, please put that away."

"Why?" I was amused by his embarrassment. I laughed, and threw it at him.

He caught the top, and immediately dropped it to the floor. The bottom landed over his face. He struggled to escape it, and dropped it to the ground, with the top.

I was hysterical at this point. It felt good to laugh. He laughed too. I was absolutely in love with his smile and laugh. I would marry him for real under normal circumstances. Whatever normal was, for people like us.

All the gifts we were sent were ridiculous. Our Domicile was filled with boxes. New ones came daily. I tried to open them all, but more came before I could get through them. The idea that the people of the Estates had this much in excess, while my people died of starvation and exposure daily was revolting. I had asked that all of what we received be donated to The Community. We kept the things they wouldn't be able to use out there, and things for the baby.

"What should we name her?" I asked Hutch one night, while we sat in the living room, having returned from dinner.

"I don't know."

"I feel like it needs to be something important sounding."

"Okay. Like what?"

"I don't know, that's why I'm asking you."

"My mother's name was Eden."

"Eden." I said it loud, "I really like that."

"Okay." He smiled. I watched him remember his mother.

"How old were you when she died?"

"I was only seven. I remember her really well, though. She was really beautiful, and always smelled like flowers. She was very strong, like you, and so smart like you too. I guess you remind me of her."

"Eden Margaret Alexander." I said it loudly with purpose.

"Perfect."

Chapter Thirty

As we got closer to the wedding, Dr. Kelly informed us we were invited to attend an Estate Assembly with her. This would be where she would introduce the rest of The Estates to The Savior Project. It was her chance to explain how her research would save them from extinction, and get further funding for it. It was more her moment than it was ours. I was not looking forward to it. It meant interacting with strangers, getting up in front of an audience, and having to answer questions about The Elements. I knew that part was inevitable, and I dreaded it the most.

I used the idea of us escaping as motivation to keep going. Hutch took to everything very easily, like Maggie when we first got there. I resisted, and she went with the flow of things. They were both happier than I was as a result.

It had been a full eight months since they grabbed me and Maggie, and brought us to The Tyson Estate. The entire time I lived inside the bubble, I wondered what it would be like to ride in one of the monorails connecting The Estates. To see what the others looked like. Today, I would.

I dressed in one of the dinner dresses they had provided for me. It was blue, soft to the touch and flowy. It made me feel pretty. I didn't know how to put on makeup, lip gloss was it. Hutch wore the same suit I had seen him in before. We looked like two completely different people. Today was a day of appointments. We were meeting with the Wedding Planner, the dressmaker, the chef, the baker, the photographer, the tailor, the florist, the DJ, a person who would play music for the party, a jeweler, a makeup artist, and most importantly, Daryl Tyson.

We met Tiny outside my Domicile, and he escorted us to the Tyson Estate Transportation Center. It was like nothing I had ever seen before. It was a hub of activity, the most people in one place I'd ever experienced. It was overwhelming.

I held Hutch's hand tight. He was apparently used to the chaos. People were wearing the bright colors, and various styles of clothing. My eyes danced. The women had painted faces and nails, the men carried briefcases. It was a flurry of activity. There was so much to see, I didn't know where to look.

We moved quickly to a waiting area for the next transport. One side for departures, and the other for arrivals. It was crowded as I felt more and more people get in line with us. There was an announcement from above, asking everyone to mind the gap upon stepping into the monorail car, and to not lean on the doors. With a loud swoosh, the monorail arrived, blowing my hair back and my dress up. The strangest part about it all was the idea of going anywhere without piles of clothes on.

We stepped in, and Tiny directed us to the rear of the car, where there was a carpeted bench we could sit on. Others filtered in behind us. They had to stand. Some leaned against the big windows, some held onto floor-to-ceiling poles to steady themselves. Others held onto straps that hung from the ceiling.

"Next stop, The Faulkner Estate." A voice rang through the whole compartment, so loud I covered my ears.

The monorail took off, pushing me back against the backrest behind me. The feeling of moving so quickly took me by surprise. It was exhilarating. I must have been smiling, because both Hutch and Tiny smiled back at me. I had never seen Tiny smile. I wasn't even sure he had teeth. I looked out the window. What I saw took my breath away. It was The Elements from above. It actually looked beautiful and peaceful. I could see the tops of the campsites. It went by too quickly for me to get my bearings. As quickly as we departed, we slowed down and stopped again.

"The Faulkner Estate" came from the speakers again.

A lot of people exited the car, mostly men carrying their briefcases and the women who were not dressed in the bright colors. A few people got on.

"Next Stop, The Taxter Estate."

This, I knew was our stop. We were meeting the dress designer for my fitting first. I felt anxious about it. Her name was Ella Luciana. She was apparently the most famous designer in The Estates. I remembered seeing her name on some clothes we found in a pull from The Taxter Estate. I'm pretty sure we tore them apart, and re-purposed them. I laughed to myself at the memory.

Again, I leaned as far as I could to peer out the windows at The Elements.

"The Taxter Estate."

I was sad it was over so quickly. A lot of people got off with us at The Taxter Estate. All the painted ladies, in their sparkly jewelry, and outrageous outfits. Some men, but mostly women. We would be meeting most of the vendors here. This was the shopping estate. All the retail stores and most of the service businesses kept their office here. I was anxious to explore, but knew we were on a fairly strict schedule.

We stepped out onto the platform at The Taxter Estate Transportation Center. It looked just like The Tyson Estate's. That was where the similarities of the two estates ended.

Chapter Thirty-One

There was too much to look at. The colors, the infinite amount of colors. My eyes darted around, not able to focus. I had to stop walking to take it all in. Hutch and Tiny clearly had seen it all before, not understanding why I needed to stop.

"Wait, I need a second." I called to them. I was actually dizzy.

"Anne, are you alright?"

"Yeah, I'm fine. Just a lot to look at."

Hutch took my hand and led me through the crowds. There were lights and signs everywhere. Dozens of store fronts. People walked about, carrying bags filled with their purchases. Sounds I had never heard before filled my ears. My heart pounded, and I was anxious to get to our destination.

Thankfully, Ella Luciana's studio was not far from the transportation center. We were only out in the chaos of the streets for a few blocks.

We stood, staring up at her name above the door. It matched the label I remember seeing.

"This is it." Hutch gave my hand a squeeze, and pushed a button next to the darkly tinted glass door.

The door slid open, and before us stood a tall slender woman with long curly blonde hair. Her eyes were gray, like the sky at dusk out in The Elements. She was dressed much more simply than I expected, in fact she looked fairly normal, save for the purple dog in her arms.

"Hello! Come in, come in!"

Inside, she showed us to a room with racks of dresses. Not just wedding dresses, but dresses in every design and color imaginable.

"I have been working non-stop since I found out about your wedding. Everyone who's anyone will be there, and they all want something cooler than banana guacamole to wear!"

I had no idea what she was talking about. Banana guacamole? She had an odd accent. Hutch looked amused by her. I didn't know what to make of her.

"Listen honey, you're going to have to leave. You are not allowed to see the dress before the wedding day."

She was talking to Hutch.

"You, tall dark and burly, you can stay." This time she was talking to Tiny.

"It's okay, Hutch, I'll be alright with Tiny. You can go."

"Tiny? Did she just call you Tiny? That's splendid." She laughed, putting the purple dog down, "Go lie down Emma, mamma will feed you later." Then facing me, "Now, let me take a look at you."

She took a step back from me, then a step toward me, then a step back again. She spun me around.

"Well, aren't you just gorgeous. Okay, have you talked to the hairdresser or makeup artists yet?"

I shook my head.

"Okay great. I love being first, so I can decide what they need to base they're designs on, instead of the other way around."

"Now, how far along are you with this very important baby?"

I hadn't thought about how much others knew about what was happening with me. "Four months."

"Well, shoot, okay. The wedding is when?"

"Three weeks."

"So even though you're a little thing right now, we have to design for the possibility of a belly."

I was absolutely fascinated by her. She was anything but normal. The way she spoke, the way she moved. The way she kept saying things were as cool as, or cooler than, banana guacamole.

She took out a measuring tape, starting with my head then shoulders, arms, chest, waist, hips, thighs, and legs. She did it so swiftly, and didn't write a single thing down, despite the pencil had clenched in her teeth.

"Uh huh, uh huh, yup." She spoke, with the pencil only slightly hindering her speech.

She spat the pencil out, dropped the measuring tape, grabbed my hand, and dragged me over to one of the racks of dresses. She slid hanger after hanger to her left, until she found the one she wanted. She took it from the rack, and place it up to my chin. She tilted her head from side to side, and frowned, returning it to the rack. More sliding of hangers, and she stopped again.

"This, this is it!"

Chapter Thirty-Two

It was perfect. Not at all what I expected her to pick for me. It was sparkly, but not ornate. It was very me.

She showed me to a small room for me to put it on, and told me to give her a shout if I needed help getting into it.

I slipped out of my blue dress, and carefully stepped into it. It was way too big. I needed help with the zipper in the back. I called out to Ella, and she was there in a flash. She must have been waiting at the door, knowing I would need help.

She zipped me up, then fiddled with the back, clipping it tight with something so the dress looked to fit me. I smiled. It was really beautiful. It had a high waist, so if my belly did grow, it wouldn't affect the fit of the dress. It was short sleeve, with a modest neckline. Layers of white satin, with a shimmery overlay and a long train down the back. It had just the right amount of shimmer and sparkle. She pulled my hair back away from my face, and magically pinned it up.

"Be right back!"

She left me staring at myself in the mirror for a moment. When she returned, she carried a tiara and a veil. She place them on me. I truly looked like a princess.

"Now that is cooler than banana guacamole! You look like royalty!"

She unclipped and unzipped me, removed the tiara and veil, then disappeared out the room. I changed back into my clothes, carefully returning the dress to the hanger, and hanging it on a hook next to the mirror.

When I came out, Ella and Tiny were talking about the next time I would need to see her, and when the dress would be ready. The whole fitting took about thirty minutes. I thanked her, and we left, to find Hutch waiting for us outside.

"How did it go?" he asked, taking my hand.

I answered, "It was cooler than banana guacamole."

Chapter Thirty-Three

The rest of the appointments went easily. Hutch made most of the decisions. I really didn't have much input, because it was all so far from normal to me. The hairdresser and makeup artists took the longest. It was so bizarre to have people touching me that way. I didn't look like myself when they were done. I wasn't a fan, but tolerated it, reminding myself of our plans. The photographer took some photos of us, I'm not sure why. That meeting was thankfully brief. He was simply thrilled he'd been chosen.

Hutch picked a simple black suit to wear. We chose blue and white flowers, and told the DJ to play whatever he thought best. And we picked simple, gold wedding bands.

Our lunch and dinner doubled as our tastings. Everything was delicious, so I let Tiny and Hutch decide what to serve. Tiny seemed excited to have a say in something. It was endearing. I picked the cake, chocolate mousse. Ella Luciana promised to pick the prettiest, but most comfortable shoes to go with my dress. Everything was set. All that was left was to meet with Daryl Tyson.

We left the Taxter Estate, taking the monorail to The Bloch Estate. From the windows, I could see fires lit at the various campsites. They looked like little orange bugs scattered throughout The Elements. We passed The Wilkes, Gilmore, and Crane Estates on the way. The only Estate I wouldn't pass through was the Winchester Estate.

Upon arriving at The Bloch Estate, Tiny warned us to follow his lead. This Estate was a lot less bustling. It was quieter, and much more subdued. Again, thankfully, a short walk from the transportation center, and we arrived at a beautiful church. The doors were gigantic, red with intimidating hardware. The heavy doors opened with a loud creak. A young man escorted us to an office at the back of the church. We walked down the aisle, wooden pews on either side of us. A large crucifix hung on the wall beyond the altar. I had never seen one so large. The windows of stained glass sat high in the walls above us. It was stunning to look at. I had been to an old ruin of a church once with Uncle Joe. I imagined it might have resembled this one when it stood.

Daryl Tyson did not look as I imagined him to. He was short, just about my height, and very thin. He wore square, black rimmed glasses, with extremely thick lenses. He wore a gray suit with a priest's collar. He had a warm smile, and a welcoming handshake. I felt instantly at ease meeting him.

"It is such a pleasure to meet you both. Please, sit down." He motioned for us to sit in the chairs across from him. He sat down at a large mahogany desk. Only a notepad and pen sat atop it. We sat down, and he took the notepad and pen in his hand.

"So first of all, I want to make sure you are both coming into this marriage willingly, not under any duress from any source."

We nodded. He wrote something on the notepad.

"Okay, excellent. I have just a few things I want to discuss, as I do with all the couples I marry."

He slid the notepad across to us, and continued talking.

"Marriage is a very special and sacred union, that should not be ventured into without great consideration from both parties..."

I stopped hearing what he was saying, as I read what was written on the pad.

We will deactivate the trackers at the end of the ceremony. The deactivation process takes about three hours, which should take you through to the end of the reception. We can't do it any earlier, or they will suspect something. You must return to your Domicile before they deactivate completely.

Hutch and I looked at each other then to Tiny. Still

talking, Daryl took the pad back in hand and scribbled more on it.

The deactivation device will be hidden in my cufflinks. I will place my hands on your shoulders at the end of the ceremony, and I will need you both to stand very still. My cufflinks will light up blue when you are clear to move.

Again, he continued to speak as we read his message. It was astonishing to me how he was able to manage speaking and writing. I couldn't read and listen to him at the same time.

"...so in closing, I am thrilled you have decided to join together, in life and love, and have asked me to perform the ceremony. Do you have any questions for me?"

Did I have any questions? Yeah, can you repeat everything you just said?

"No, I think we're all set." Hutch answered for both of us.

I wasn't completely clear on why Daryl was helping us, or how he had the tech to disable the tracker. I asked Tiny as much on our way back to The Tyson Estate.

He explained that he and Daryl grew up in The Estates, learning about their grandfather Calvin Tyson, and he would not be happy with the way the Colonists have lived so lavishly and frivolously, destroying what he built to save mankind. In his original vision, we should have been able to house everyone under these bubbles, not just the super-rich. Everything that has happened here is a disgrace to our grandfather's legacy.

"We thought they would waste it all and perish, and then they started The Savior Project. I signed on, so I could watch what they were doing.

"At first, they simply studied The Elements, and took samples of the earth out there, to see if we could find a way to grow vegetation. They set up cameras to study The Commons, and see what you were doing to

231

survive. When they started bringing the Commons into the Combine, I contacted Daryl. I told him everything I knew about what was going on, and told him about the trackers.

"I got him one, so he could figure out a way to disable them, so we could free The Commons they were studying. As it turned out, a lot of your kind liked being there, despite the trials. Daryl and I thought it could be great to be able to bring The Commons in. But not all First Gens are created equal, Annie. Hutch, you should know this. The trials they put you through determined whether or not you were what they needed. If you don't make the cut, they send you back out. That was not the case with you. You and Maggie, they found what they were looking for in you two, and Malakai."

Hutch flinched hearing his name. I did too. I could see Hutch remembering.

"Then I saw what they were going to do to you. I didn't act fast enough to get you all out. They pumped

Malakai up with all that testosterone, steroids and human growth hormones. I wish I had seen him that day. I didn't let him into your Domicile that night, Annie. I need you to believe that. Dr. Sanford did."

"What? Why?" I asked, completely thrown by his whole story.

"To see what would happen. To see if they could orchestrate a Second Gen."

"That's disgusting." I spat, completely appalled.

"I contacted Daryl after everything happened. After I brought Hutch out to your campsite, I thought I would be able to get you out too, but they induced your coma, and I couldn't move you. Then, they did the unthinkable. When you woke up, I was going to get you out then, but you insisted we bring Hutch back here, so I had to come up with another way to get you guys out, and this is it."

"Thank you Tiny. For everything."

I was exhausted by the time we got back to The Tyson

Estate. My feet hurt, my face hurt from smiling, my throat was raspy from talking. My mind was tired from everything Tiny told us. I was very relieved to be back in my Domicile, and fell asleep almost immediately upon my head hitting the pillow.

Chapter Thirty-Four

The Estate Assembly would take place a week before the wedding, in The Wilkes Estate, the only place large enough to house the amount of people who wanted to attend. We were just a day away from it. I felt like every minute of everyday leading up to it was planned out for me, with final dress fittings and meetings with vendors. I got so used to taking the monorail, and the chaos of The Taxter Estate. It was becoming my normal, and I hated it. I couldn't wait to get out.

The plan had us escaping on the wedding night, when we were promised to be left alone, without cameras, or anyone watching us, as requested by Dr. Kelly herself. It was working out perfectly.

We knew we couldn't take Maggie with us, and with what Tiny had said, there wasn't any hope she would ever wake up. It broke my heart to leave her, but we truly had no choice. We decided we would come back for Maggie when Tiny determined things were settled enough, so we could bury her out in The Elements, where she belonged.

"Hey," I said, trying to get Hutch's attention. He was reading quietly next to me.

He looked up at me. "Yes?"

"I'm glad we're getting married."

"Me too," he said, with a confused half smile.

"I just wanted you to know that."

"What's up?"

"Nothing, I'm just tired, I guess. I feel like everything is happening so fast. Soon little Eden will be here, and everything is going to change." I looked at him, hoping he understood what I couldn't say out loud.

"I know." He answered, understanding.

I placed his hand on my stomach. "Can you feel that?"

Eden had the hiccups.

"Yeah, that's neat."

"It's crazy how much she moves around now."

"I can only imagine how strange this must all be for you. You are incredibly brave, Anne."

I didn't say anything after that. We sat in silence for a while, before going to bed in our respective bedrooms.

Tomorrow would be a big day.

Chapter Thirty-Five

The ride to The Wilkes Estate was slow. People got on at every stop. I knew every single one of them was coming to the assembly. Each estate brought more people, and brought me more anxiety. Hutch and I sat. Tiny, Dr. Kelly and Dr. Sanford stood, holding one of the poles. I was happy we got to sit.

Once we got to The Wilkes Estate, it was a mass exodus at the transportation center. We all filtered out, and walked to the Great Hall. Tiny told me it used to be called Madison Square Garden. It could hold up to 20,000 people. There was a stage, and a podium set up in the center of a large oval of seats, that rose for what seemed like miles to me. It was the most people I had ever seen in my life, let alone all in one place. The sound of the crowd was booming.

We were escorted by two men in dark suits to the stage. Dr. Kelly stepped up to the podium. She tapped the microphone attached to the podium. It let out a squeal that silenced the entire crowd.

"Ladies and Gentleman, thank you so much for joining us today. My name is Dr. Madeline Kelly."

I had never known her first name. It was funny upon hearing it. I thought to myself, 'she doesn't look like a Madeline.'

'We are so pleased to present to you The Savior Project."

An uproarious applause startled me. I didn't know how loud a group this large could be.

"As you know, our home is in danger. The earth is running out of resources to sustain our climate controlled estates. For the past year, we at The Savior Project have been searching for a solution, a physical solution, that will allow us all to live independent from our artificial environments. To live outside these bubbles, before it's too late. Today, we are the closest we have ever been. Here to my left is my co- founder,

Dr. Timothy Sanford."

Dr. Sanford stood up, to applause.

"To my right are two very special people. Please meet Anne and Hutch. Anne has come to us from out in The Elements. Hutch is the son of Dr. Edgar Alexander, a researcher with us in The Tyson Estate."

Hutch stood up and waved. I followed his lead, waving awkwardly, my eyes to the floor, feeling the eyes of thousands boring into me. I knew they would be fascinated to see someone from the outside. They cheered enthusiastically. It seemed like an eternity before we sat down again.

"Our research has discovered an evolutionary phenomenon in the people born inside these bubbles, and more importantly, outside these bubbles. Our studies have shown the anatomical makeup of some born out in The Elements, First Gen Commons, has evolved to survive out in those harsh conditions. At the same time, our First Gen Colonists have also evolved.

"I will spare you all the scientific mumbo jumbo we get really excited about, and get to the good stuff, the important recent developments.

"We invited a group of Commons to join our research."

Invited? I thought to myself. There was no invitation. We were kidnapped, and dragged against our will into a prison. That was her first lie.

"We have studied how their bodies respond to life in the Estates, and the results were extraordinary. When taken care of, fed, and rested properly, they were stronger, faster, and smarter. Not all First Gen Commons experienced the same evolution. The most advanced came from two subjects, sisters. Anne who is here with us today, and her younger sister Margaret who, because of her young age, couldn't be here with us today."

And that was lie number two. I was trying desperately

to keep my emotions in check as I listened to her.

"Upon arriving at our facility, Anne and Margaret were horribly malnourished. We nursed them to health, and discovered their evolution was vastly accelerated, compared to their fellow First Gen Commons."

I felt my fists clench. Nursed us back to health? I shook my head. Hutch gave me a look of concern and warning. I relaxed my hands.

Dr. Kelly pulled up a graphic on a huge screen behind us. It was a picture of the two scans she had shown me, when she explained to me why I was so important.

"Here we have a side by side comparison between a First Gen Common, and one of our Colonists."

She went on to explain the differences. There were murmurs, and sounds of shock and amazement coming from throughout the large audience.

"So, now for the most exciting part."

You could hear a pin drop. The entire audience of thousands were at the edge of their seats, hanging on her every word. Dr. Kelly took a moment, letting the anticipation grow.

"We have successfully implanted a Second Gen embryo. One made up of a First Gen Common, and a First Gen Colonists. Meet the parents of our savior!"

She gestured for us to stand. The applause and cheers were deafening. I could feel the rumble of the Great Hall in my chest. The whole place literally shook.

Hutch smiled, and waved. Again, I was uncomfortable, and awkward. I mimicked Hutch's smile and wave. Once the cheers died down. Dr. Kelly continued. What she said shook me to the core, harder than applause from a crowd of a million could have.

"We have also successfully implanted Margaret with a Second Gen Common. Because she is so young, we are monitoring her closely. Both miracle children are due in a little over five months."

More thunderous applause.

There was no hiding the look of shock on my face. Hutch was equally shocked. He grabbed my hand, and held me in my seat. He knew I was about to pounce on Dr. Kelly.

"Now, I know you probably have many questions. Because of the size of this group, we will not be taking questions today."

She went on to share contact information, and announced a series of visits to all the estates, to answer questions they may have.

I was shaking. How could she? Maggie too? And Malakai as the father. I was certain now they had put us both in comas to be incubators, and never intended for me to wake up. They sent Hutch away, so he couldn't protest, and here we were. Flaunting and celebrating the complete and total violation they've committed on me and Maggie.

Perhaps sensing my brewing fury. Dr. Kelly quickly wrapped up, and left the stage. Dr. Sanford followed her, leaving Hutch and I behind. The crowd started to break up, and rush the stage. They were screaming my name, and asking questions. Tiny came out of nowhere and rescued us, steering us away from the encroaching mob. The fear of getting trampled trumped my wrath towards Dr. Kelly. We got out relatively unscathed, and made our way back to the transportation center. Dr. Kelly and Dr. Sanford were nowhere to be found.

Once we were on the monorail, Hutch spoke first.

"Anne, I know you're upset. I am too. They had no right."

"Did you know about this?" I looked accusingly at both Hutch and Tiny.

"Of course not. How could you think that?" Hutch answered, looking hurt.

"I knew." Tiny said quietly. "I knew, but there was nothing I could do about it, and I thought it would make your leaving easier. They might leave you alone, if they know they have Maggie."

I didn't know what to say. Even though Tiny was helping us, there was so much awful he was responsible for, and took part in. I felt defeated.

"We have to continue with our plan, Anne," Hutch said. I knew he was right, and of course he didn't know what they were doing with Maggie. He was out in The Elements when they did everything.

"There is no way they are going to believe that I have nothing to say about what we just learned."

"She's right, Tiny."

I was happy Hutch agreed.

"Okay, what do you want to do?"

"I want to kill her."

"Well, we know that's a bad idea."

I sat silently, staring out the window. The monorail was empty, since everyone was still at the Great Hall.

I felt Eden move. I hated what they were doing to Maggie. In an instant, I knew what I needed to do.

Chapter Thirty-Six

After confronting Dr. Kelly, so they wouldn't suspect anything, we started packing for our escape. Nothing major, just Element appropriate clothes for both of us, and some rations of food. We didn't want to carry too much. It would just slow us down. My meeting with Dr. Kelly was brief. She didn't even let me speak before she apologized for my finding out that way.

"I know it must have come as a shock to you about Maggie. We didn't know the paternity of the successfully implanted embryo until a couple of days ago."

"She's just a baby herself."

"Anne, Maggie isn't going to wake up. She is not really here with us anymore. I know it's hard to accept, but we need her like we need you."

"You're using her! And you're using me!"

I kept willing myself to calm down, but the rage kept bubbling to the surface.

"Please try to understand how important you both are, and that what you're a part of will help everyone, not just the people in here but your people too. It's for the greater good."

I had to balance between not conceding too soon, and not ripping Dr. Kelly's head off. I kept reminding myself we just needed to get through the ceremony, successfully deactivate our trackers, smile through a reception full of strangers, and get back to our Domicile within the three hour window.

Easy.

Not really.

The idea of going out into The Elements with Hutch and now a baby was terrifying. Would I remember how to live out there? Would Hutch be okay? Would I be able to have this baby out there? So many questions. The only thing I was sure of was I did not

249

want to be part of The Savior Project, and be poked and prodded. I refused to let them stick needles in me, Hutch, or our baby, for them to say it's for the greater good.

We spent the next week behind the artifice of the wedding, while preparing for our escape. There were a lot of notes passed between us and Tiny. The trips out to the Taxter Estate were important, as it gave us the time we needed to speak freely with Tiny. When we were in our Domicile, we could escape to the bedrooms, but never for too long, so as not to raise suspicions. Being pregnant, on top of everything else, was exhausting. And it seemed my stomach was getting bigger everyday.

Hutch was sweet and attentive. They had stopped making me do anything. I was to eat and rest and take care of myself. It would have been nice, if there wasn't everything else I had to worry about.

Before we knew it, the wedding was upon us.

"Are you nervous?" I asked Hutch.

"A little. Are you?" We both knew we weren't talking about the wedding.

"Extremely."

We were sitting on the couch in our Domicile. Hutch took my hands in his.

"It's all going to work out. It has to." I could tell he was choosing his words carefully.

I squeezed his hands, then placed one on my belly and said, "for her."

Chapter Thirty-Seven

The person in the mirror was a stranger to me. She looked strong and beautiful. She wore a stunning white dress, tiara and veil. Her hair was lush, swept up in a perfect crown of curls on top of her head. Her face looked fresh, healthy and alive with pale pink, shiny lips. In her hands she carried a bountiful bouquet of flowers in white and blue. On her feet, she wore a perfect pair of white ballet slippers. I smiled at the girl in the mirror, knowing I would never see her again, and I was completely fine with that.

"Are you ready?" It was Ella Luciana.

"I think so."

"They're waiting for the guest of honor. You look like royalty."

"It could be the crown." I joked.

"It's cooler than banana guacamole. Let's go."

Ella was wearing a pantsuit, with an almost obscenely plunging neckline, in bright orange. Her matching shoes had dangerously high heels. Her lips and hair matched her outfit. She looked ridiculous and gorgeous all at the same time. Out of all The Colonists, I would miss her the most, after Tiny, of course.

We walked up to the church. Ella carried the train of my dress. Tiny would give me away. I was told traditionally the bride's father would do that, and I didn't want anyone but Tiny to do it. If Uncle Joe had been around, it would have been him.

Upon reaching the giant red doors, they opened, anticipating our arrival. I could see all the pews filled, and more people standing in every possible free space in the church. There were some onlookers outside the church, but they were thankfully kept far away from me.

Tiny looked handsome in his gray suit. He proffered his arm, and I slipped my hand through the crook of his elbow. I started to tremble. You could see the movement in my flowers.

"Breathe, Annie. You look beautiful."

Music started to play, and all the people sitting in the pews stood up. I could see Hutch standing at the front of the church with his father. He looked incredibly handsome. This was it. I took a deep breath and exhaled. Everything was about to change forever.

There was a gasp from the crowd, as I stepped into view. The photographer and his assistants were snapping pictures of me. Ella fanned out the train of my dress behind me with pride, then remained at the back of church, while Tiny and I made our way up to Hutch and Daryl Tyson.

The trip down the aisle seemed infinitely longer than the last time I had gone down it. We passed stranger after stranger. Their smiles were eerie to me. They were probably nice people. I never wanted to find out.

The way Hutch looked at me as I approached was

worth all of the nonsense we went through to get there. Despite everything, I was happy to be his wife.

I watched him get emotional. His lip quivered, and his eyes moistened. He took a deep breath, and exhaled loudly, trying to compose himself.

Tiny left me at the altar, shook Hutch's hand, gave a nod to his cousin, winked at me, and took a seat in the front pew behind me.

"Here we go," I whispered to Hutch.

He didn't respond. He wasn't doing a great job composing himself. It made me smile.

We looked up to Daryl Tyson. He stood on a step above us. Holding his hands in the air, he motioned for everyone to be seated.

"Dearly beloved, we are gathered here today to witness the union of Anne and Hutch..."

His voice trailed off, as I lost focus on him, and looked at Hutch. I remembered everything that had happened, since the first day I met him. The insanity that brought us to this very spot. The insanity that would follow. I caught sight of Daryl's cufflinks. They were green. I was trying to remember what color he said they needed to be when we had to hold still. Was it green or blue? I decided to hold completely still just to be sure.

He droned on and on, about love and marriage, and the importance of communication, and keeping God present in our home and life. I had no idea what he was talking about. I was concentrating on his cufflinks. Then he took my hand, and Hutch's hand, and faced us to each other. Tiny handed him the wedding bands. I forgot all about that part. We exchanged rings. I put Hutch's on him, and he put mine on me. We were holding hands. Then we were asked to speak.

"Do you, Hutch, take Anne to be your wife, to have and to hold, in sickness and in health, until death do you part?"

"I do."

"Do you Anne, take Hutch to be your husband, to have and to hold, in sickness and in health, until death do you part?"

"I do."

"It is with great pleasure, and honor, I pronounce you husband and wife. You may kiss the bride."

Hutch looked at me. I was biting my lip. I couldn't believe I had to kiss him in front of these people. He cupped my face in his hands, and brought my lips to meet his. We kissed softly, and sweetly. If not for the circumstances surrounding us, it would have been perfect.

There was a huge cheer, and applause. Daryl put his hands on our shoulders and gripped us tight. That was our cue not to move. We looked to each other, then to Daryl's cufflinks. They were blinking red. We stood completely still. Was there something wrong? He never said anything about red. It felt like hours before the light turned blue, and he released his grip on us. We stood up straight and faced the crowd, which was still cheering.

Chapter Thirty-Eight

We basically ran out of the church. There were people lined up outside, throwing rice at us as we exited. It was a silly tradition. We played along, laughing as we shielded ourselves from being pelted. I had gathered my train up, and slung it over one arm. It was heavier than I anticipated. We kept running the few blocks to the transportation center. We were promised a car to ourselves, and we got one. It was me, Hutch and Tiny.

"Here. This is a master key. It opens every door in The Estate."

"Every door?" I asked.

"Yes, every door. But it's mine."

"So they can track it back to you." Hutch added, taking it from him, and placing it into the interior pocket of his jacket.

"Yes. I will figure out how to explain that when the

time comes. Don't worry about me."

"You could always claim we took it from you." Tiny shot me a look as if to say, 'are you kidding? They would never believe you could get anything off me.'

"Now all you have to do is make an appearance at the reception. Here." He handed Hutch a timer. The time was counting down already. "I hit it as soon as the cufflinks went blue. This is how much time you have to get back to your Domicile. I will do everything I can to make sure you get out of the reception with enough time to get back, before the deactivation is complete."

We arrived at The Taxter Estate. Inexplicably, Ella Luciana was there to greet us.

"Alright, my adorable newlyweds, time to greet your public!"

We stepped out of the transportation center. The entire estate was transformed into one giant party to celebrate us. Hutch looked at his timer. We had two hours and thirty-seven minutes to get back.

It was an endless sea of faces looking up at us. We didn't have time for all of this. We walked down to our table for dinner. People passed us, saying hello, wanting to touch us. I was kissed and hugged by dozens of people, before reaching our table. I made Tiny sit with us. He would now act as our bodyguard. A rainbow of colors flashed by us, over and over. I was certain Ella had dressed them all. The music was loud. People were dancing about, drinks in their hands. Some seemed to have been drinking for a while. It was absolute chaos to me.

We were brought our food. We ate quickly, between visits from strangers. Then we had to fulfill the various traditional activities everyone was expecting. We had our first dance. I tossed my bouquet. We cut the cake, took about a thousand pictures, danced some more. If it wasn't for the fact that we were running for our lives in a couple of hours, it would have been a lot of fun.

"Make an announcement. You guys have to go." Tiny whispered to Hutch.

Hutch stood up with a glass and a knife, and started tapping the glass to get everyone's attention. I thought he would have to break the glass to be heard over all the noise.

"Hello everyone. Thank you so much for coming out to celebrate with us. Unfortunately, we have to get going."

There were disappointed moans, boos, and grumbling.

" Please feel free to continue the celebration!"

That was met with enthusiastic cheering.

"Anne is tired," I feigned a yawn, "and I have to get this lovely lady home."

There were more cheers, and some grumbling. Tiny quickly lead us through the crowd, back to the transportation center. It was eerily empty.

"Okay, this is it. You have thirty minutes to get to

your Domicile. Dr. Kelly is waiting for me to let her know you are back, at which time she has promised to go dark on your room. The next time I see you will hopefully be the last for a long time."

We hugged the big man. It was strange to think by this time the next day, we would be free of this place.

We hurried back to our room. We plopped down onto the couch, and started to snuggle. We were playing the part of newlywed, for anyone who might be watching.

"Welcome back, you two. Congratulations. I will see you in the morning. Have a wonderful night."

It was Dr. Kelly's voice. We heard a bit of static and then the familiar hum of our room went silent. She did as she promised. No cameras or microphones. I felt the slightest vibration behind my ear, just as the timer Hutch was carrying started to beep.

It was time.

Hutch and I quickly went to work. We changed out of

our wedding garb. We pulled our bags out of their hiding places, and waited for Tiny. For a long moment, we stood there holding our breath. Then Tiny knocked.

No words were exchanged. We hurried past him, and down the route we had practiced. The exit we targeted took us right past Maggie. We memorized the route on our daily visits to her, so we wouldn't need Tiny to escort us. He needed to be free to handle disabling the cameras as we made our way out. We were on our own.

We crept silently down the metal corridors, our breathing the only sound. We were approaching Maggie's room.

"Wait! We have to see Maggie."

"Anne, we don't have time."

"Hutch, I'm going to see her. You can come with me or not, but I'm going."

Hutch, stopped running and returned with me.

"This wasn't part of the plan." He warned.

"It was part of mine."

Chapter Thirty-Nine

Closing my eyes, I held the cable plugged into the wall in one hand, and Maggie's hand in the other.

"Anne, we have to go," Hutch whispered urgently.

"I know," I answered, annoyed. I had to remind myself it wasn't Maggie lying there anymore, It was simply a vessel, carrying a solution. She would never wake up from her coma. She would never be the same Maggie again.

I squeezed her hand. "I'm so sorry little one. I love you."

I ripped the cable from the wall, ripping my heart out with it. I was crying uncontrollably, still holding Maggie's hand.

The machines went silent. I could see her chest stop rising and falling. I watched the life completely leave her little body. And a large piece of me died right there with her.

Hutch was at my side, trying to gently pull me away.

"C'mon, Anne. She wouldn't have wanted you to get caught."

I leaned down and kissed her cheek. She was still warm. I looked at her one last time. She looked peaceful.

Grabbing Hutch's hand, we ran out of the room. I didn't look back. I couldn't.

We found our way to the Emergency Exit, and used the key Tiny gave us to get through the door, alarms sounding as we did. The wind and cold hit us immediately, taking our breath away.

We ran. We ran until our lungs and legs burned. It was unbearably cold. My body wasn't used to The Elements anymore. The clothes Tiny provided were no match for The Elements. We needed to find better clothing.

The ground was hard, the snow crunched with every step. Low hanging branches whipped and tore at our faces. I could feel the warmth of blood on my face freeze on my cheeks. I let go of Hutch's hand to wipe it away.

"Anne!" Hutch suddenly screamed.

I turned to face him, and he was gone.

"Hutch!"

"Anne, down here!"

I ran back to where I knew him to last be, and found a hole. A hole in the ground. Hutch had fallen down into it.

"Are you okay?" I shouted down to him. I looked behind us, and could see the lights of the Staties, coming after us.

"Yes, I think you should come down here."

"What? No, we have to go, the Staties are coming!"

"Anne, listen to me. Jump down."

I hesitated a moment, then jumped down to meet him. The drop was about eight feet. I landed hard, but upright. What I saw around me, I didn't believe. What I felt, I believed even less.

Chapter Forty

It was warm. Hot even. We were in what looked like some kind of supply closet. There were hundreds of unlabeled silver canisters. There was warmth coming from a vent in the wall. A flickering light above us hissed, and we heard sounds outside the one door in the room.

"Did you hear that?"

It sounded like a child.

"Yeah, do you think we caught one?"

Hutch and I looked at each other. What could they be talking about? Why were there children there? I had so many questions running through my head.

"Caleb! Get away from there."

It was a woman's voice.

"You know you're not allowed back there."

"Sorry mom. C'mon, let's go, we'll sneak out later and see what we caught."

There were shuffled steps, and then silence.

"What is this place?, I asked Hutch, knowing full well he wouldn't have an answer.

We waited in silence a while longer, then decided to try opening the door, the Staties in pursuit of us forgotten.

The door had a knob on it, not like the doors in the Tyson Estate I had grown accustomed to. This was like the doors we found in the rubble of The Elements. The metal knob was warm to the touch. It turned easily, and opened into a hallway.

I was scared, but needed answers.

Hutch took my hand, and we ventured out into the dimly lit hallway. Silently, we explored.

It looked nothing like the hallways in the Estate. The walls were white, the floors carpeted and spongy under our feet, in complete contrast from the ground above. I smelled food. We didn't dare talk, and give ourselves away to whoever was there.

We moved along to the end of the hallway. My heart was pounding. Still holding hands, we walked out into a large room. It was empty. We heard voices, and then laughter. I looked at Hutch. He looked like I felt. Confused, scared, hopeful.

"Hello?" Hutch was looking up, and shouting.

"What are you crazy?" I whispered.

"They don't sound dangerous. It sounds like a family."

He was right. It did sound like a family. A family sitting down and eating dinner. An image I had only seen in books and magazines I found with Uncle Joe.

They heard Hutch, and were instantly silent. We heard someone coming, and I braced myself ready for a fight.

"Who's there?" It was a man's voice, but to my surprise, he didn't sound angry.

"We're lost, and we don't mean any harm." Hutch's voice echoed through the empty room.

The man entered the room with a look of confusion, not malice.

"I'm Hutch, this is Anne. We sort of fell into your closet from above ground, and found our way out here."

I kept waiting for the man to yell at us to get out. I still didn't fully understand where we were.

"You two must be freezing. Come, come in."

I looked at him, wide eyed. He was not angry we were there. He was welcoming us into his home.

We followed him, dumbfounded. If we had accidentally fallen into an Estate, or onto an unknown Pride's Camp, we would have surely been fighting at this point.

He led us into what looked like a kitchen. The food we smelled was laid out on a large table, with a woman and two young boys sitting at it. They looked like us, with a slight difference I couldn't quite pinpoint. Their skin was pale, their eyes were giant, a bright ice blue. Their lips were an almost unnatural pink. They were very thin. They all looked up, and smiled at us.

I was thoroughly and utterly confused. In my whole life, there was no such thing as a warm welcome. This was the definition of one, and I had no idea how to take it. I had so many questions. What was this place?

In my mind I called it The Underground.

Preview - One Season Book Two: The Underground

"Uncle Joe?"

Anne ran ahead of me, to a man I didn't recognize but I knew from her stories of him. It was our first venture out since we settled into our Dwelling in Sub Terra, what we still called The Underground.

"Annie?"

He recognized her immediately. They embraced warmly. Turning to me with smiles, I felt their eyes on me and I suddenly felt uncomfortable.

"This is Hutch, my husband."

"Husband? What? I can't believe you're old enough to be married!"

He shook my hand firmly. Almost too firmly.

"It's kind of a long story." I watched Anne regale basically her whole life to her long lost friend.

I sat, quietly listening as they caught up.

I wasn't entirely sold on whether or not Joe was a friendly, or if I should be suspicious of his motives.

He took us around the market, and introduced us to more of the Sub Terra Dwellers.

He welcomed us into his home, where we met his wife Magda, and children Matthew and Joe Jr.

Their space was similar to the accommodations we were given. I was still unclear why everyone was so nice. I am not normally a cynic, but I found my head crammed with negative thoughts I couldn't shake.

Anne wouldn't understand. I was the one who pushed for us to journey down here. I insisted we stay until the baby was born. I was beginning to second guess our decision.

Sub Terra and its Dwellers was turning out to be more of a mystery the more we learned.

* * * * *

One Season Book 2: The Underground will be available in Summer 2019

Made in United States
North Haven, CT
08 July 2023

38704107R00150